In Praise of *Bedroom Feng Shui*

"Clear Englebert's book *Bedroom Feng Shui* is a thorough, insightful and charming reference for anyone wh[...]
principles in the bedroom. Beginn[...]
anyone interested in feng shui!"

Author of *Wind and Water*

"Hit the alarm and wake up to a new you by following this book's advice!"
—Karen Rauch Carter
author of *Move Your Stuff, Change Your Life*

"The bedroom is perhaps the only really private space we have at home and thus needs the attention that only feng shui can provide."
—Nancilee Wydra
Popular American Feng Shui author

"A thorough, level-headed evaluation of the often infuriating complexities of the extraordinary Asian philosophy called feng shui. *Bedroom Feng Shui* provides unfettered access and fresh detail to the intricate ins and outs of intimate feng shui."
—Dennis Fairchild
Author of *Healing Homes: Feng Shui—Here & Now*

bedroom
FENG SHUI

CLEAR ENGLEBERT

THE CROSSING PRESS
FREEDOM, CALIFORNIA

For information on bulk purchases or group discounts for this and other Crossing
Press titles, please contact our Special Sales Director at 800/777-1048, Ext. 203.

Visit our Web site: **www.crossingpress.com**

Library of Congress Cataloging-in-Publication Data

Englebert, Clear
    Bedroom feng shui / by Clear Englebert.
        p. cm.
    ISBN 1-58091-109-9 (pbk.)
    1.Bedrooms. 2. Feng shui in interior decoration. I. Title.
NK2117.B4   2001
747.7'7--dc21   2001042385

0   9   8   7   6   5   4   3   2   1

Contents

A Note to the Reader

This book introduces feng shui concepts and tools that may be unfamiliar.

Almost anything can be a feng shui tool if used skillfully. Some things are so commonly used, they have become associated with feng shui—crystals and mirrors, for instance. The bagua is a special tool for feng shui, and has been given its own chapter.

CHAPTER ONE

Feng Shui and the Importance of the Bedroom

WHAT IS FENG SHUI?

The words are pronounced "fung shway," and they mean *wind/water*. Feng shui is the Chinese art of placement. It originated in the mountains of China between three and five thousand years ago. It is popular because it works. Feng shui offers a system of arranging furniture and objects to assist you in accomplishing your goals and reaching your highest potential.

The old Taoist masters of China greatly respected nature. It was their teacher, and learning from nature is endless. All of nature including the movement of wind and water is considered to be an expression of *chi* energy.

CHI ENERGY

Chi is the basic energy of the universe. The concept of chi energy is easy to grasp if you think of it as energy that gets your attention. A car with flashing lights and a blaring siren attracts a lot of chi energy because it is extremely noticeable. Heads turn, and energy is required to make those neck muscles work. This is one aspect of chi energy. A wind chime has the same effect. When people hear it, they often turn their heads.

Some of the things that attract chi energy most strongly are light, brilliant color, movement, sound, and stunning beauty. The advertisers of the world learned these lessons long ago. That's why television commercials often attract your attention more than the program.

To understand how chi energy flows inside your home, be aware of what gets your attention first. For example, if the first thing you notice in a room is a clean, bubbly fish tank, that's good. It probably puts a smile on your face and makes your eyes light up. But if the first thing you notice is a window with a distant view, you may be smiling, but your attention is miles away. One of the goals of feng shui is to keep your attention gracefully flowing around a room. The chi should be sweetly meandering.

Your home has vibrant chi energy to the degree that it feels vibrant. If the first thing you notice in a room is how cluttered and full of furniture it is, then the chi energy is stagnant. A bedroom should feel restful. A multifunctional bedroom may have to be used during the day, but at night you should be able to change it easily into a restful mode.

As another way to consider how chi flows, think about how you are able to move within a space. For example, think about a long hall that allows you to move quickly, like a bullet from a gun barrel. The bullet is harmful, and so is the speeding chi energy. The ideal traffic pattern of energy in a room is gently curved; you should be able to reach all areas without having to cautiously step over or around objects.

Think of yourself as an example of chi energy because that is what you are. How you feel within a space is a good indicator of how chi is flowing there.

THE IMPORTANCE OF THE BEDROOM

According to feng shui, the bedroom is the most important room in the home. If you sleep eight hours per night, that's a third of twenty-four hours; therefore a third of your life is spent in that room. In general, you spend more time in the bedroom than in any other room. Therefore the more time you spend in a particular room, the more influence that room has on your life. This applies even if you are asleep—the room is still affecting you.

Universal agreement is a rare thing in feng shui, and some feng shui authorities maintain the kitchen is the most important room in the home because the food that fuels a person's life is prepared there. Both rooms are very important, but kitchens are not always as important as they were a hundred years ago. The introduction of modern conveniences such as microwaves and dishwashers means less time is spent in the kitchen preparing food and cleaning. Also, people now eat in restaurants more often than in the past. The kitchen can be a very important room, but not when it's used mainly to heat something in the microwave occasionally. Some people literally never cook, and for them the kitchen is just a place to store a few containers of prepared food.

People aren't all the same, and they never will be, but almost everyone sleeps in their bedroom. I've had only one feng shui client who ignored her nice bedroom and chose to sleep every night on the comfy couch in her living room. Some people do that on an occasional basis, but this woman did it every night. After she told me where she slept, I ceased emphasizing her bedroom and reevaluated her living room.

CHAPTER TWO

Location of the Bedroom

Some parts of a home are better places for bedrooms than others. Even if you have no choice about the location of your bedroom, it is still important to know what factors may be affecting you due to its location. The first factor used in feng shui to evaluate the location of the bedroom is the concept of *yin/yang*.

YIN/YANG

Everything that exists is classified as primarily yin or yang. Nothing is totally yin or totally yang. Everything is on a scale—more yin or more yang.

Yin	Yang
Lower part of a room	Upper part of a room
Private	Public
Moist	Dry
Dark	Light
Complex	Simple

continued next page

Yin	Yang
Female	Male
Cold	Hot
Soft	Hard
Quiet	Noisy
Round or oval	Square or rectangular
Indoors	Outdoors
Matte finish	Shiny or glossy

Imagine the floor plan of your home or draw it if that's helpful. Then draw a line through it from side to side. The rear half of a home (based on the formal front door as the front) has a more relaxed energy than the front half. That energy is called *yin*. The front of a home has a more active, or *yang*, energy. You don't always have a choice about where your bedroom will be. But if you do, pick a room at the rear of the house. The energy there is conducive to deeper rest.

The front door of your home is referred to as the "mouth of chi." It partakes of an active energy even if a side door is more commonly used in everyday life. If your bedroom is in the front of the house or close to any street, I suggest a fairly heavy window treatment. Venetian blinds alone are a bit skimpy in this case. It would be better to have sheers in the daytime and heavy, sound-absorbing drapes (like velvet) at night.

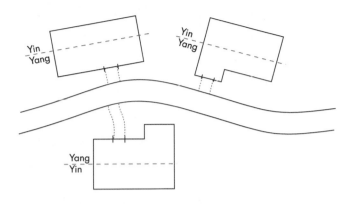

The yin and yang (front and rear) of a house

BEDROOMS EXTENDING BEYOND THE BULK OF THE HOUSE

If a bedroom protrudes beyond the bulk of the house, it has a feeling of separateness. If you sleep there you will probably not feel as connected to the rest of the household as you would in a bedroom located within the main shape of the house. In this case, a mirror is used on the wall of the bedroom that connects it to the main body of the house. The mirror should face into the bedroom. If putting a mirror on that bedroom wall is not an option, then look to the illustration for examples of other walls in the home that

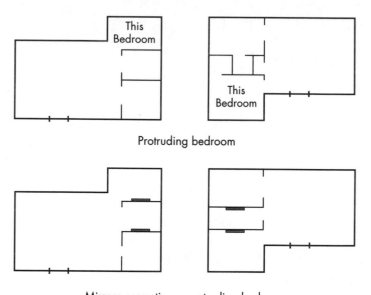

Protruding bedroom

Mirrors correcting a protruding bedroom

should have a mirror. Only one wall needs a mirror, whichever one works best in your situation.

Mirrors can simulate the effect of a window. When looking into that window, the extending bedroom is seen within the main part of that house. The mirror symbolically pulls the bedroom into the main body of the house. The mirrors in the illustration would reflect the bedroom if some of the walls were gone. The walls do not have to disappear to serve their feng shui purpose.

BEDROOMS AND GARAGES

If a bedroom is located directly above a garage, you may not get your best rest there. The car has a very active come-and-go yang energy, and it is too close to the place where sleep energy should be emphasized. To aid restful sleep in this situation you can put very heavy solid objects on the floor of the bedroom. Two examples would be a sculpture or a table supported by a marble base.

You can hang a crystal over the car in the garage. This can be done even if the garage door opens upward—use your ingenuity.

You can put a mirror (any kind, any size) on the ceiling of the garage, reflecting the top of the car. Alternately, a very small mirror could be put under a rug or carpet in the bedroom, facing down toward the car.

As is often the case in feng shui, more is better. If it is possible to do all three things, then do so.

If a bedroom is directly behind a garage, there is a similar problem, because the "metal beast" is pointed directly at a sleep area and undue pressure could be felt in your life. Place a mirror on the back wall of the garage so it reflects the front of the car away from the bedroom. A reversed mirror could also be put in the bedroom with the reflective side pointing at the wall and at the car on the other side. A mirror in the garage is preferable to the reversed mirror in the bedroom. If you must face the mirror to the wall, cover it somehow so it doesn't look weird. The garage is no problem for sleepers if cars are never parked in there.

KITCHEN OR BATHROOM
IN RELATION TO BEDROOM

If a kitchen is located directly over a bedroom, a small mirror should be placed on the ceiling of the bedroom, reflecting down. The mirror symbolically seals off and reflects back the bustling kitchen vibrations from the quiet bedroom. The mirror can be quite small—even one inch in diameter will work. Such mirrors are available in craft and hobby stores.

There should always be a door between the bedroom and the bathroom. The door should always be kept closed at night when sleeping. The moist energy of the bathroom should not be able flow around you during your dream time. If you own the home, put in a solid (not louvered) door. If that isn't possible, put up curtains, even sheers. The curtains can stay open until sleep time.

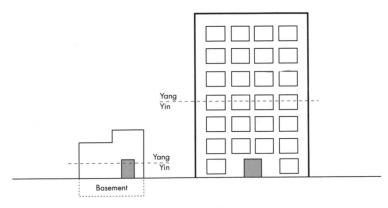

Vertical yin-yang of a building

HEIGHT OF THE BEDROOM IN THE BUILDING
Basement

If the bedroom is in a basement or at ground level, it has the advantage of being in a yin location, because it is low in the building. The main disadvantage of this location is that the lowest rooms in a building (especially a building that is more than four floors high) have a vibration of "pressure" because the bulk of the space is above them. It is fairly easy to fix this bit of oppressiveness by using light.

The best type of light fixture for a basement or other low room is an *uplight*, one that aims the light up such as a torchiere or wall sconce. Light is energy and when it strikes the ceiling it symbolically pushes it up and away, thus relieving pressure. The simplest uplight is a can light, a type of directional spotlight that is in effect "a light bulb in a can." They are inexpensive and available at hardware and lighting supply stores.

I generally recommend clear light bulbs for any type of uplight as long as the bulb is not seen by the eye. The force of the light is a bit more yang and powerful than with frosted bulbs. Also, if it looks appropriate (or is completely unseen), use some kind of pointy bulb, such as a flame tip. That way, even the shape of the bulb is symbolically pushing away the pressure from above.

A clear light bulb makes distinct shadows. You can take advantage of this by using floor lights to illuminate plants from below. This projects shadows of natural forms and beauty onto a surface that is fairly plain in most homes. By putting light and shadow onto the ceiling, you are subtly activating the yang part of the room. Subtle is appropriate because the bedroom does not benefit from too much yang energy.

If the main light of the room is one light bulb in the center of the ceiling that aims down, you can convert it into an uplight by using a silver-tipped bulb. Then, the light that reaches you will have been reflected off the ceiling. Silver-tipped bulbs may not be appropriate in every instance. If it makes the room seem dimmer,

Standard bulb on ceiling   Silver-tipped bulb on ceiling

it may not be the right kind of bulb for your situation. It depends on what other kinds of light are in the room. It is usually best to paint ceilings white or pastel because light is reflected better. A dark ceiling often feels oppressive, as if chi is bearing down.

Ground floor

Bedrooms on the ground floor are extremely common and fortunately, they don't pose any feng shui problems unless there are more than five floors above them. If there are many floors above them, uplights would be called for. Use them as you would in a basement situation as described in the previous section.

Bedrooms on the ground floor (as well as basement bedrooms) can benefit from having a fairly light-colored floor or rug. This is frequently the case in rooms with many floors above them. The lightness of the rug lifts the energy of the room. In a one- or two-story house, however, that is probably not a concern.

Up to Four Floors

Bedrooms on the first four floors of a building do not have any inherent feng shui problems based on their height in the building. It's nice to be able to say that, because that's where a vast number of people sleep.

A problem in some modern homes is the proximity of electric wires. If you can look out your bedroom window and see electric wires within 30 feet, you may have a problem of strong electromagnetic radiation. See page 70, for more information on electromagnetic fields.

Four Floors High and Beyond

Bedrooms that are quite high in a building benefit from having at least one (and preferably several) very heavy objects in the room. A heavy object (such as a large stone sculpture or a marble table) acts as a solid grounding force. The bigger the better, without being too extreme. Heavy objects work best if they are placed low in the room—on the floor.

A high bedroom should have some heavy and substantial-looking furniture. Darker furniture (such as walnut) is preferred to light (such as bird's-eye maple). The bed, especially, should seem well-connected to the floor.

If there's a carpet or rug, it should be somewhat dark. A white or very light-colored rug is too airy, and has "float-away" energy. The darker floor color is more grounding.

High-rise bedrooms are a fairly recent invention in the history of humanity. There is another fairly recent invention that helps counter the negative effects of sleeping so high up—a magnetic mattress pad. It usually fits under the regular mattress, and provides an even, negative magnetic field for the body. More information on these mattress pads is on page 40. Although magnetic mattress pads are especially useful in high-rise bedrooms, you do not have to live in a high bedroom to enjoy their extra restful effect. There are several fine manufacturers. One is Magnetico, in Calgary, Alberta, Canada (800-265-1119, www.magneticosleep.com).

CHAPTER THREE

Location of the Bed

For some people the title of this chapter will elicit the comment, "As if I have a choice!" In some bedrooms there is no choice. Only one wall looks and feels right for the bed. Anything else would simply not work.

It is important that where you sleep feels right. Intuition plays a vital role in the placement of the bed, but there are also feng shui rules that should be observed. It is helpful to know the reasoning behind the rules.

EMPOWERED POSITIONS

As chi enters a room, it brings with it the aspect of that which is new. When you are aware of the door, you are aware of what is coming into your life. If you are able to see the door (without moving your head more than ninety degrees), you have empowered yourself and strengthened your natural extra sensory perception. If you can't see the doorway, you have disempowered yourself and set yourself up for surprises.

The number one rule is to be able to see the door easily from the bed. The door represents the future. When lying in bed with your head propped up on a pillow, you should be able to see the main door into the room. If you have to crane your neck to see the door, you are setting up a dynamic in your life that can cause things to surprise you. Events will seem to come out of the blue, and you won't be prepared for them.

Sometimes it is too awkward or impractical to place the bed in the correct position. In this case, use a mirror to see the door. Put the mirror at such a height and angle so if you are lying in bed, the reflection of the doorway is plainly visible. In some instances, that means angling the mirror so that it looks bizarre.

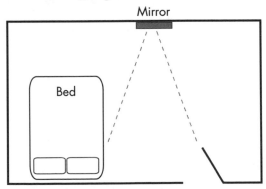

Mirror placement to see the door

In that case you might want to consider using a convex mirror or a large gazing ball instead. But you should not use a convex mirror to check your hair or see how your clothes look. If you use a convex mirror, try to arrange things so you won't be tempted to use it for that purpose. Seeing yourself in a mirror is akin to knowing yourself. If your reflection is distorted, it will be more difficult for you to have a true awareness of who you really are. Gazing balls are excellent alternatives and fit well in many decors. They are silvered reflective balls intended for use in a garden. Nicely mounted, they look great indoors. They even come in beautiful colors. If you use a colored gazing ball, be sure it is just as reflective as the silver ones.

WINDOWS AND SKYLIGHTS

The bed—especially the head—should not be directly next to any window. Locate the bed elsewhere in the room. If that can't be done, just make sure that a heavy window treatment is used each night. Windows that are several feet away from the bed are not a problem.

Skylights are wonderful, but do not sleep directly under one unless there is some type of pull shade covering it at night. It is considered to have a "wide open and out there" quality. The quality that enhances deep sleep is more "tucked back and sheltered."

TOILET

Do not place the bed so that the head of the bed is on a wall with a toilet on the other side. If there is no other choice, put a mirror behind the bed. The reflective side of the mirror should face the wall. The mirror does not have to be visible.

If a toilet is directly above a bed on the next level up, put a small mirror on the ceiling with the reflective side pointing up. Try to locate the mirror directly under the toilet.

CEILING

If the bedroom ceiling slopes, the head of the bed should be under the high part of the slope. Placing the head of the bed under the low part of the ceiling adds pressure to your life. The area under the high part of the ceiling is good because there is a natural expansiveness and simply more air.

There is a way to symbolically correct or level any sloping ceiling. This becomes especially important if the bed cannot be placed in its most ideal location. Hang a faceted prismatic crystal from the high part of the ceiling to the level where the wall meets the low part of the ceiling. A red thread is considered ideal for hanging the crystal, but in many decors a clear monofilament looks best. Hanging the crystal is the main thing. It would also be a good idea to state your intent at the moment of hanging the

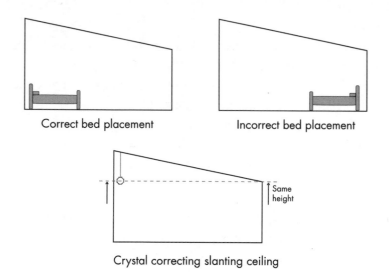

Correct bed placement

Incorrect bed placement

Crystal correcting slanting ceiling

crystal: "I am hanging this crystal to symbolically level the ceiling" or any other words that seem appropriate. You are not really changing the level of the ceiling. You are doing something symbolic, and therefore your intention comes into play very strongly.

BEAMS

Exposed overhead beams are considered to "beam down" a pressurized energy. They are responsible for holding up the structure, and there is indeed pressure on them. That pressure influences the energy of the room as long as it is seen. All structures have beams, but in most cases the ceiling covers them. As long as they are covered, they are not influencing the room.

The exposed beam only causes a problem if it crosses directly over the bed or a favored lounge chair in the bedroom. If there is no option but to locate a bed under an exposed beam, it is necessary to make the beam go away—at least symbolically. You can do so by removing the beam if it is not structural, or you can hide the beam so that its shape is not apparent. Use fabric. In some situations it works to have strands of tiny clear lights behind the fabric. The effect is similar to seeing stars through a mist. If lights are used, turn them off when sleeping. You can make the beam visually disappear by painting it the same color as the ceiling. If painting is not an option, hang a crystal or wind chime over the bed or chair. Bamboo flutes are also a popular option for dealing with problem beams. Use the nine-inch thread method as described in the bamboo flutes section below.

Bamboo Flutes

There is a special way to hang bamboo flutes. Using red ribbon cut to nine inches or a multiple thereof, hang the flutes at a forty-five degree angle with mouthpieces down and toward the walls. The red symbolizes blood and represents a new beginning, or new blood foundation. Red is a powerful color in feng shui and can influence change. The number nine is the highest single-digit number. This conveys strength and can symbolize the strength of the intention. The intention in this case is whimsical, yet works well. The uplifting sound that a flute can produce helps raise the beam and relieve pressure.

This red-ribbon technique can also be used for hanging items like wind chimes or crystals anywhere.

Sometimes a beam lends itself to having a plant (real or artificial) trail along it or twine around it. It is especially important that the lower part of the beam is covered. Uplighting, such as a wall sconce or torchiere, can counter the beam's effect if placed directly under it. A mirrored tabletop placed directly under the beam reflects the beam and lessens its detrimental effect.

DOOR

Generally, chi energy enters a bedroom (or any room) predominantly through the entrance door. There is a swath of strong chi energy about three feet wide (the width of the door) going directly across the bedroom—from front wall to back wall. Make sure the bed is not located in this swath of energy. This particular energy packs a punch, and hopefully there is a way to locate the bed out of its path. It is particularly important not to lie fully

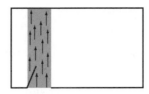

Strong chi from doorway

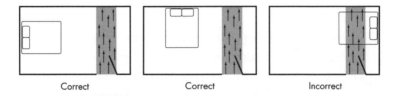

Correct   Correct   Incorrect

Bed placement relative to chi from the doorway

within the swath of chi energy with your feet facing the door. That is known as the coffin position because coffins are carried through doorways feet first. If there is no choice but to have a bed located in that swath of energy, some sort of buffer or screen should be placed between the door and the bed. Examples are:

- An armoire or large chest
- A folding screen
- Tall, thickly foliaged plants (even good artificial ones will do fine)

- A curtain—preferably thick like velvet, but even sheers will work.
- A beaded curtain, if that works with the decor.
- A thick, patterned rug.

If none of the above or anything similar is appropriate, just hang a crystal.

Crystals

The crystal symbolizes the intention to deflect the overly strong chi energy and prevent it from hitting the bed. Just as the facets of a crystal can cause light to reflect in many directions, a crystal's facets symbolically disburse energy. Be sure the crystal is hanging between the door and the bed, above head height. Hang the crystal with red thread or ribbon if it looks appropriate; otherwise, use clear monofilament. This symbolic kind of feng shui solution is made stronger by expressing the intention out loud or in thought. Say whatever seems appropriate. "This is to deflect the chi from the door," or "I wish to sleep more soundly." Use whatever words feel right to you. Intention expressed is intention strengthened.

The thread or string should be cut to nine inches or a multiple of nine, but it does not matter how low from the ceiling the crystal hangs. Hang it a bit low, but not in the way, as they chip easily. Lead crystal is softer than glass, so be careful handling it. A chipped crystal will still make rainbows, but it will forever be a chipped crystal and not ideal for feng shui purposes.

CHAPTER FOUR

The Bed as a Physical Object

HEADBOARD

A good solid headboard can do two things. It helps bind a relationship, and it represents backing. Even if the bed is not a relationship bed, it is still important to have a solid headboard (not bars or slats). A solid headboard can instill more confidence in your life by reinforcing the feeling that your decisions are backed up. If the bed is a relationship bed, the solid headboard does more than provide backing. It symbolizes a solid unity. You should be able to look at the headboard and say, "That's how I feel about our relationship, honey—solid!" Bars or slats (or any headboard with holes in it) represent an open relationship. They are not considered to be conducive to monogamy. If having a solid headboard isn't possible, then intertwine the bars or slats with ribbon, fabric, or strands of silk plants.

Headboards are generally made of wood, metal, or fabric. They sometimes incorporate materials such as leather or mirrors. Because a solid headboard is ideal in feng shui, I recommend wood. Wood is sturdy and solid and brings those qualities into the life of the sleeper. Wood is more yin and conducive to rest. It also has a friendlier feel; it is not as hard and cold as metal. Solid metal headboards are probably available, although most metal headboards are composed of bars. However, metal is too yang and shouldn't be close to the head during sleep. Padded fabric is not my first choice, but it is certainly not a bad option. There is usually some solid wood on the back side, and fabric has a restful, yin quality.

There are diverse opinions concerning mirrors in headboards. See page 66. If you don't already have a mirrored headboard, I don't recommend getting one. If you already have one and don't feel that you are getting your best sleep, try covering it at night and see if you notice a difference. Cover it for at least a month to know for sure. If you have a mirrored headboard and sleep quite soundly, then I doubt it is having an adverse effect.

Be wary of headboards that have a high overhead shelf built into them. Preferably, put nothing on that shelf (over your head) except perhaps plant vines twining together. The plant pots should not be in the area over your head, but off to the side. No heavy objects, such as books, should be on the high shelf. Also be wary of a headboard with an extremely angular design, such as the one in the illustration above. It is too fiery and active.

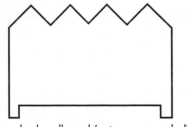

Angular headboard (not recommended)

If you don't want a headboard or cannot get one, consider a headboard substitute. A quilt or other heavy fabric hung from the wall at the head of the bed is a reasonable substitute. It won't be quite as good as a real headboard that is attached to the bed, but if a dark fabric is used, it will sure seem solid.

FOOTBOARD

A footboard represents grounding. If there is no footboard on the bed, your feet will symbolically hang out in space for a third of your life. This can add spaceyness to the personality. The footboard should be approximately the same height as the top of the mattress. If it is too high, as in sleigh beds, it has a confining quality. The footboard should always match the headboard in design and materials.

Of course, a lot of beds are designed to have a headboard only—no matching footboard. If a footboard is not an option, try placing a cedar chest, a bench, or even a dark-colored blanket at the end of your bed. A dark rug on the floor at the foot of the bed is another simple solution.

MATTRESS

Whatever mattress size is comfortable and appropriate is okay with feng shui. However, the box springs of a king-sized bed usually consist of a pair of twin-width box springs, which can be a problem. This is inappropriate for a relationship bed because it represents a separateness. The box springs are closer to the floor than the mattress, and are therefore more fundamental. Such a situation reinforces the fundamental differences between the two partners. Swapping the bed for a queen-sized bed is a perfect solution, because it also draws the people physically closer together. If that isn't a workable solution, get a red king-sized sheet and place it between the box springs and the mattress. Try to find a brilliant red sheet, because it will symbolize a new "blood" foundation. If the king-sized mattress is on a platform and there are no box springs, there is no problem. Be cautious when using an old mattress in a new relationship. Many people let go of the old mattress on a relationship bed when new partners are sleeping there (or when anticipating a new relationship). For some people, it can be important to part with the entire bed. Letting go of old things in our lives opens up the way for new things—and people—to flow in.If keeping the old mattress is the only option, then clean and air it well. Also, do what's called clearing. It is usually done for a whole room, but it can be done effectively for any object. Waft incense all around the mattress quite heavily. Speak boldly and assertively, saying something like, "Any old vibes must get out now," or whatever feels appropriate. It is cleansing on a vibrational level and is quite effective for restoring the original vibrational purity of a thing or a space. More information on Space Clearing is on page 149.

Mattress Materials

A box spring and a mattress of some kind on top of it are what most folks sleep on. This type of setup usually is some distance from the floor, and that's good. Low beds are not a feng shui favorite. There is a vastly improved model of the ordinary bed called Dux. The mattress is a very thin pad, and most of the comfort and support is from the unique box spring. They are not cheap.

Foam mattresses are not a problem unless they have come brand-new from the factory. When foam is new, it can release gaseous chemicals into the air. Once the foam is a few weeks old, the problem usually ceases. If you smell a chemical odor coming from a new foam mattress, that's the cause. Just expose it to excellent ventilation (i.e., fresh air) for the first few weeks. Don't sleep on a new mattress that has a strong chemical smell. If a foam mattress is used, be sure that the underside is well ventilated by turning it over regularly.

Cotton futons are natural and comfortable for some people. They are, however, too firm for others, especially those who sleep on their side. A cotton futon must have good ventilation beneath it or be flipped over regularly. If you live in a damp environment, watch out for mildew.

Some people love waterbeds, and some people never will. If sleeping on a waterbed feels restful and intuitively right, then do it. But make sure if partners sleep on a waterbed, they both should feel benefited. A water bed is a large amount of water in a big bag. There are five archetypal "Elements" in feng shui, and Water is one of them. Pages 94-95 explain which kinds of things represent each element. The area around a waterbed benefits from having things that represent the Wood, Earth, and/or Fire elements. In this way the Water element is reduced, and the area is more balanced.

An air mattress is rarely a good permanent mattress. The sleeper's body causes the bag of air to be pressurized, and that pressurized vibration continues throughout the night. Use an air mattress only when it is necessary, as when camping.

Magnetic mattress pads are a fairly recent invention, based on the concept of magnetic therapy. Magnets are embedded at regular intervals in a pad. The pad then goes under a standard mattress, but not under the box spring. I don't know about the spectrum of magnetic therapy products, but I do know when I rest well. I'm a light sleeper and I appreciate the quality of rest when sleeping on a magnetic sleep pad. They are expensive, but good sleep is priceless. I especially recommend them for insomniacs. More information is found on page 23.

UNUSUAL BEDS
Foldaway Beds
Foldaway beds are a marvelous design solution for multipurpose bedrooms. The feng shui verdict is mixed, however. The good news is, because they are put away in the daytime, they retain restful vibrations. Ideally a foldaway bed is one that is out of the living space in the daytime. The bad news is that they are usually

vertical all day long, and that symbolizes alertness. It's a fairly minor problem, though. A foldaway bed is definitely preferable to a bed that is in the way all day and is used as a couch. A mattress that folds into a couch is not bad, but has more yang vibrations than a bed that disappears.

Bunks and Trundles

Bunk beds are not ideal. Unless the sleeper is a child, bunk beds are usually temporary, for example, when staying in a cabin. In a dormitory-type situation, there is a feeling of impermanence, of wanting a room of one's own. This is not conducive to sound sleep. If bunks must be used, the structural supports beneath the upper mattress (the metal links or wood slats) should not be visible to the person in the lower bunk. Perhaps a fabric with a star pattern can be used to cover it. Children sleeping in a bunk bed should be able to sit up in bed without bumping their heads. If that happens, they've outgrown the bunk bed, and it's time to look for different sleeping arrangements. To energetically open the space above a bottom bunk, hang a tiny bell or put a map of the stars under the upper bunk, facing down. Some feng shui teachers recommend that bunk bed occupants trade top and bottom bunks occasionally.

Trundle beds have no inherent energetic problem. The lower bed gets tucked away in the daytime and retains restful, yin vibrations. The upper bed may or may not have some yang energy, depending on how much it is used as a couch in the daytime. Be sure the trundle moves in and out easily. When children use trundle beds, sibling rivalry can be an issue.

Sleeping Lofts

There are two kinds of sleeping lofts. One is a huge piece of furniture that provides living/work space below the upraised bed. This situation calls for attaching a small mirror to the bottom of the bed, reflecting down onto the most active workspace, i.e., directly above the desktop or computer monitor. If you work in the space below the bed, you should not have an exposed structural beam of the bed above you. Cover the beam with fabric, or see other solutions on page 28. A loft bed (and some upper bunks) can be too close to the ceiling. You should not be so close to the ceiling that you bump your head when sitting upright or you cannot move around easily.

An architectural sleeping loft is a semiprivate high room. At least one wall is open to the larger portion of the house, and the area may have a balcony railing. Such openness in a bedroom can be a problem. An obvious factor is whether or not sounds can be heard coming from the rest of the home at bedtime. If you can make the loft more quiet and private at night, then do so. Curtains or Roman shades are possible options.

Many sleeping lofts put the occupant very near a slanted ceiling. The head of the sleeper should be under the high part of the ceiling. In a loft, the high side is usually the side that has the entry. The concern here is that the bed needs to be in an empowered position. The person in the bed must be able to see the person entering and the bed must not be in a direct line with the entry. Use a mirror if necessary, as described on page 24.

Both kinds of lofts are commonly entered by climbing a ladder. A ladder usually does not have risers connecting the rungs or steps. An open ladder fails to completely guide chi up to the bed area. Worse things have happened, but it isn't ideal. Steps with risers are great, according to feng shui, but an attempt to visually "fill in" the riser could result in a dangerous and awkward-looking situation, so it is probably best to leave well enough alone.

Floor Sleeping

If a mattress was designed to be placed directly on the floor, then do so. But if a mattress was intended to be up on a frame, then it should be on one. A standard box spring and mattress should always be off the floor and have a skirt (or something) to connect it visibly to the floor. Sleeping on the floor may be grounding, but there is a better quality of chi a few feet higher in the bedroom.

Chest Beds

A chest bed has built-in drawers to maximize storage areas. However, the ideal feng shui bed should store only items that relate to the bed, such as pillows and neatly folded sheets and blankets. If other things must be stored under the bed, those things should be emotionally quiet. No old tax records, no old diaries. Clothes and bedding are less of a problem, because they get laundered regularly, washing away old vibes. It's better to store soft things under a bed, rather than hard things like tools. If hard things must be stored there, put a very small mirror under the mattress facing up under the bed. The mirror can also be under the mattress support, accessed through the drawers.

Canopy Beds

Canopies can make you feel secure or claustrophobic. Don't sleep in a claustrophobic space if there is any way to avoid it. If a canopy makes you feels secure, then restful sleep will inevitably occur. Some canopy beds have a high structural support that crosses over the sleeper. Try to cover the support with fabric in a way that hides the shape of the support. If it can't be seen, it's not there, is a handy feng shui trick. If the central support must be seen, it should have a rounded, faceted, crystal hanging from it. A small disco-ball shaped lead crystal is best.

Any bed with four high posts, one at each corner, needs rounded posts. The square posts can cause what is known as "poison arrows." See page 54.

Hammocks

A hammock can provide a restful nap, but is not ideal as a permanent bed. If slept in night after night, a hammock can cause back problems. There are two types of hammocks: those with a wooden stretcher at the head and/or foot of the webbing and those with no stretcher. A hammock with a wooden stretcher is secure only as long as you remain in the middle of the hammock. It is very easy to fall out of this type of hammock. Those without a wooden stretcher feel safer because they usually do not have a tendency to turn over and cause the occupant to fall out.

BED CLOTHES
Bedspread

Fabric is yin, because it is soft and flexible, not stiff and hard, which is yang. But some fabrics are more yin (velvet and chenille, which are fuzzy) and some fabrics are more yang (a slick, shiny satin or metallic cloth). A soft, textured bedspread is a good feng shui choice. The color can be determined by which area of the bedroom's bagua the bed is in. See pages 110-111. If the bed is a relationship bed, try to use warm colors (such as a dusty rose) to symbolize a warm relationship.

It is a good idea to love your bedspread, or at least be very fond of it. Often it is the dominant fabric in the room. If you love your bedspread, making your bed each morning won't seem like such a chore. The bed should be made shortly after rising. Then the old "sleep energy" won't be affecting you when alertness is needed during the day.

It is best not to be able to see under a bed—use a bed skirt or something similar. The bed is more grounded if the floor under it is hidden from view.

Sheets

Soft cotton sheets are ideal in my opinion, perhaps flannel in cold weather. The soft coziness of flannel makes it a perfect yin sheet. If the bedspread is doing its job, the sheets are not seen when the bed is made. Therefore, the sheets could be a color that enhances the area of the bedroom according to the bagua map (as referenced under "bedspread" above). If that idea appeals to you, go for it. If it is a relationship bed, both partners must be content with the color selection. Because they are so yin, black sheets are extra restful. They represent quiet night. Solid color sheets are visually quieter than most printed sheets and are generally a better choice.

Pillows

Pillows must be comfortable and healthy for your neck. There are many different kinds of pillows, and manufacturers of all of them claim great benefits from the use of their pillows. Use your own judgment. How well do you sleep, and how does your neck feel in the morning?

Feng shui cares more about how many pillows are on the bed. Too many pillows amount to clutter. An overabundance of decorative bed pillows is a decorating fad. Try not to have pillows that are purely decorative on the bed. If you must, a few are all right. It is better to like the look of the pillows that are actually used. It's fine to have a bedspread cover all the pillows if there are only one or two. The pillows are then tucked away and remain more yin.

Blankets

Natural material is preferred for all bed clothing, including blankets. Electric blankets are not recommended, even if they are not plugged in. Electric blankets influence a sleeper's body whether they are turned on or not. The range of effects is:

- The blanket is plugged in and turned on. Even a small electric current is disruptive to the body's own natural electrical workings.
- The blanket is plugged in, but not turned on. This is still not great, because there is a direct connection between the blanket and the electric system of the building.
- The blanket is unplugged but still on the bed. Because the connection to the wall is broken by unplugging, this is quite livable. Many people turn on an electric blanket before getting into a bed to make it warm and cozy and then turn it off. It is best to unplug the blanket, not just turn it off. It is also ideal to remove the electric blanket before going to bed. It would be better not to have the metal wiring so close to your body for a third of your life. To avoid all of this, just use a hot water bottle.

CHAPTER FIVE

What Happens in a Bed

People do more than just sleep in a bed. What takes place on or near a bed leaves a karmic residue that can affect the quality of sleep there.

SLEEP

The primary purpose of a bed is sleep—any other purpose is secondary. The ideal situation is a bed that is used for sleep and nothing else. Not everyone has that luxury, but if the bed can be used only for sleeping, then do so.

Come sleep time, a bedroom needs to seem like one giant sleeping pill, a space that supports nature's blessed rest. Whatever else happened on or around the bed should feel long gone.

You get your most restful sleep when three factors are fulfilled. Total darkness. If window light can be totally blocked, then do so. Some people will always want a night light, and if so, use the lowest wattage available (three watts or less). Dollhouse lights are extremely low wattage and are appropriate in some situations—

especially where the light is on a small protective or spiritual image.

Total quiet. Noise at night is a big problem in certain places. My condolences to you if your bedroom is disturbed by noise. It can make the world a more hateful place. Make your bedroom more quiet by using a lot of heavy fabrics. Otherwise, use earplugs or pillows to muffle noise. Use a masking device (such as a fountain or "ocean sound" machine) only when necessary, because it adds to the noise level, albeit minorly. Your deepest sleep occurs on the quietest nights.

Light air circulation. The ideal is a very light, fresh breeze wafting over you. If noise is not a factor, try to leave a bedroom window at least slightly open at night. Hardware stores sell safety devices to secure a slightly open window. Don't use a fan unless you must, because of the extra sound. However, if you need a fan to remove stagnant chi during the hot summer months, place it as high as possible and try to hang a crystal from the base of the fan to disperse the cutting energy of the blades.

It is important to know that our deepest, most restful sleep occurs before midnight. If you go to bed earlier, you will awake more rested. Also, do not eat just before going to bed.

Dreams are an aspect of sleep. They can be important learning tools in our lives. I recommend keeping a pad and pen by the bed (or a tape recorder) to write dreams immediately upon awakening while the details are fresh in your memory. (See Recommended Reading, *The Dream Book* and *Dreams* audiotape, both by Betty Bethards.)

SEX

Whatever happens sexually in your bed is you and your partner's business only. Some lovemaking is gentle and quiet (yin) and some is boisterous and exuberant (yang). If your lovemaking tends to be boisterous, consider making love someplace other than the place you sleep. There will be a yang vibration lingering on what should be a rather yin bed (for the most restful sleep). People who think of themselves as light sleepers can be disturbed by such vibrations more than someone who falls asleep easily and stays asleep throughout the night.

If people don't live with you (or with you and your partner), you can move any very boisterous lovemaking from your bedroom into a different room. Do so only if it feels right. The bedroom will then be more conducive to deep sleep.

EATING

Do not eat in bed on a regular basis . If you truly have no alternative, then be sure to spare a moment at the beginning and end of each meal to be consciously grateful for the nourishment. The two moments of gratitude formally begin and end the meal. The ending gratitude allows the bed to resume its prime purpose—rest.

COUCH SUBSTITUTE

If your bed must serve as a couch substitute, as in many small studio apartments, that's too bad. However, it is not often a very serious concern in the scope of the whole bedroom. If the bed must serve as a couch substitute and you sleep quite soundly, it is probably not a big deal. If you don't sleep well, try to find a way to put the bed away—even if that means getting a bed that will fold into a couch.

Do not begrudge the extra moments it takes to fold the bed away. Done mindfully, these moments add centering to the day. Then, when the bed is set down for sleep, the mindfulness is an introduction to dreamtime. On page 47, I suggest you don't use an excess of decorative pillows on the bed. Only when the bed functions as a couch substitute is it all right to go ahead and use lots of pillows, if that's your style. Pillows (or any decorative fabric like a tapestry or afghan) act as a symbolic buffer between the mattress that is slept on and the couch that has a more active use.

CHAPTER SIX

OTHER FURNITURE

Bedroom furniture with curves is usually preferred to hard-edged furniture. It is more yin, and yin is most important in bedrooms.

This is not the room for glass tabletops because they are very hard and shiny. Glass is a form of metal. It is yang, and better kept to a minimum in bedrooms. Stone tabletops are also very hard and yang. Wood surfaces are better in bedrooms because wood is a more yin material.

POISON ARROWS

One of the main concerns with bedroom furniture is whether or not it is causing a poison arrow, and whether that poison arrow is crossing the sleeper's body.

A poison arrow is a line of chi energy that has picked up a negative charge by encountering a sharp right angle. Poison arrows are most often caused by furniture with sharp angles along the vertical edges. To see the exact path of this kind of poison

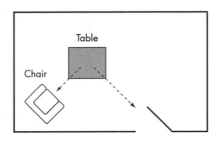

Poison arrows

arrow, divide the sharp angle in half and follow where it points. If it points out into a space that is only walked by, or rarely sat in, there is no problem. But don't have this type of poison arrow (coming from a sharp right angle) pointing directly at the entry to a room. It is subliminally saying no to people who enter, and it is also saying no to chi energy.

A poison arrow can be stopped by draping the offending edge with fabric. It can also be stopped by placing a substantial object (such as a large plant) between the sharp edge and the bed. If the vertical edge of the furniture is well-rounded or is an angle larger than ninety degrees, as with a six-sided table, there is no poison arrow.

You spend up to a third of your life in bed. A third of your life should not be spent in the path of a poison arrow. The stress of

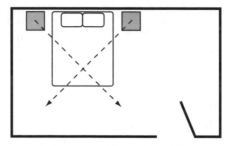

Poison arrows from side tables

being constantly in the path of a poison arrow can manifest as a health problem. The area of the body that is in the poison arrow's line becomes more vulnerable.

SIDE TABLES

Bedside tables can make some serious poison arrows point across the bed. If the side table aims a sharp right angle across the bed as in the illustration above, consider getting side tables with rounded corners. If the side tables with sharp right angles must stay, cover them with a tablecloth. If a tablecloth won't work, put a piece of fabric (towel, shirt, or whatever) over the offending corner when you go to bed for the night—every night. If there are extra pillows on the bed, stuff them between the poison arrow and the bed.

Side tables should be about the same height as the bed—not drastically lower or higher. Matching side tables are ideal for a relationship bed.

DRESSERS

Dressers have two kinds of potential problems. They can cause poison arrows if their vertical edges are sharp, and they can have mirrors that are a bit on the low side. It is important that the mirror show all of your head when you're seeing your reflection. If the mirror cuts off the top of your head when you are walking around the room or standing right in front of it, the mirror needs to be raised. In a couple's bedroom, the mirror should not cut off either person's head.

CHESTS OF DRAWERS

A chest of drawers must not point a poison arrow at the bed. It must not seem foreboding by being overly large and dark for the room. If it has a mirror, the same rule applies as with dressers—the head must be fully seen.

ARMOIRES

Everything in the above section applies to armoires. If there is adequate closet space, don't even have an armoire, unless it is used to store a television. Even more than a chest of drawers, an armoire can have a foreboding presence if it is large and the room is small. If the room is small, it is imperative that the armoire be made of light-colored wood and have graciously curved edges.

CHAIRS

If there is a chair in the bedroom that is frequently used, place it so that the occupant can see the door to the room. Any chairs in the bedroom should seem inviting—soft, warm, chairs are preferred to bare wood or cold leather. If it works in the decor, have the color of the chair be the correct bagua color for its placement in the room. See page 95. If the main bedroom chair is a desk chair, it is good if the back of the chair fully covers the occupant's back. It represents solid backing in life.

BOOKCASES

Do not have a bookcase in a bedroom unless necessary. Books have a noisy yang vibration because of all their words. If they need to be in the bedroom, they must not dominate the decor. Downplay them. Ideally, put them in a bookcase with doors. In some situations it works to cover a bookcase with fabric.

There is a second reason for covering a bedroom bookcase. If the bookcase is directly facing the bed, the edge of the shelf is sending a cutting energy across the sleeper's body. It is a form of poison arrow, but it can be quite nullified by putting a real, from-the-earth crystal (such as quartz) on any shelves that are approximately at the same height as the mattress top. Crystals often have sharp points and those should be pointed away from the sleeper's body. I usually direct the crystal points upward. If the shelf boards are extraordinarily thick (1-½ inches or thicker) there is much less danger of a poison arrow coming from them.

The vertical edge of the bookcase must not aim a poison arrow across the bed.

DESKS

A small decorative desk that is seldom used is not a problem in a bedroom as long as there is plenty of room for it. An active desk that is used for hours each day is a different matter. Such a desk retains its active yang vibrations. If the desk must be in the bedroom, try to screen it from the bed. Some desks screen themselves by having a roll top or fold top. This type of desk is ideal if the surface is closed away when the work is through. If nothing else will work, just drape decorative fabric over the desk busyness while sleeping.

CHAPTER SEVEN

Other Things to Consider in the Bedroom

WINDOWS

The ideal window in feng shui is one that opens fully and completely. Windows, like doors, allow chi to enter your life. Windows that open fully allow you to reach your potential more easily. The vitality of fresh air is chi energy. Let it into your bedroom. Do not have windows that rattle or are painted shut. Windows should be fully functional, otherwise there can be a dysfunctional tendency that isn't easily overcome. Also keep your windows clean. Clean them at least twice a year. Windows represent your inner eyes, your ability to know what you should be doing in your life. Clean windows allow you to do that more fully.

Hopefully the view is pleasant outside your bedroom window(s). If it isn't, consider installing a window box with plants. They are easy to install and transform a view quickly.

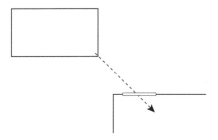

Poison arrows from neighboring building into bedroom window

From your bedroom window, you should not see a building (or other large object) pointed directly toward you. The following illustration is an example of that situation. If there is any sharp or foreboding building or object pointing at the bedroom window, put a mirror outside to exactly reflect the building (or object). A convex mirror is ideal, because you don't have to aim it exactly. The bulge of the convex mirror reflects more of the view. If there is a very busy road outside the bedroom window, definitely use a convex mirror to reflect more of the road. If the mirror cannot be placed outside the window, put it inside the window facing out. It should still reflect the foreboding object and be as close to the windowpane as possible. It is fine to use a small mirror. If a church, mortuary, or cemetery is directly next door and visible from the window, put a mirror outside to reflect it.

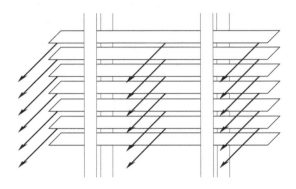

Poison arrows from Venetian blinds

Do not leave bedroom windows bare! Use some kind of window treatment. Drapes and curtains are better than Venetian or vertical blinds because fabric is softer, and drapes and curtains cannot aim a blade of cutting energy into the room.

Blinds can easily slice up the air in a room with lots of cutting energy. Each louver is a symbolic blade. Trace the path of that blade into the room to see where the slice is aiming. Adjust the louvers so they do not aim their blades at you when you spend time in your bedroom. It is not important how the louvers are aimed during the time the bedroom is not in use (i.e. during the day for most people).

Heavy window treatment does not appeal to everyone, but I believe it would appeal to more people if it didn't seem to cost so much time or money. Good, heavy window treatment is the job of a professional or someone (you?) willing to learn. Heavy means thick material, lining, and the following items, if they appeal to you. If done well, they can make a bedroom a true nest as nothing else can. You can add:

- Valance—this is almost a must
- Tassels
- Fringe—especially very thick, long fringe
- An excess of fabric

The fabric excess can be done with lots of folds—even in the valance, if it looks good. It can also be done through pooling the drapes on the floor. Feng shui loves the pooling because it symbolically gathers the lower chi and directs it *strongly* upward.

Don't rule out heavy window treatments for the bedroom until you have exposed yourself to some good examples of its use. There is an abundance of fine books on window treatments. One such book is *Winning Windows* (see Recommended Reading).

If heavy window treatments don't appeal to you, perhaps something modern like heavy Roman shades would work. If it is difficult to obtain the desired degree of darkness in the bedroom, consider installing a blackout roller shade behind the more decorative window treatment.

When a bedroom window is directly opposite the door to the room, the chi that enters the bedroom is likely to vanish quickly out the window. Sheer curtains will keep the chi in and allow it to circulate within the room. A small decorative mirror is also a good idea. Place it on the wall above the window, facing into the room. It symbolically reflects the chi back into the room. Also a decorative object such as a crystal, wind chime, or mobile can be hung from the ceiling between the door and the window.

DOORS

A door, even a cabinet door, can aim a poison arrow into the room. To see how this kind of poison arrow can happen, see the following illustration. Wherever a door points to in a room is where the poison arrow is pointing. The solution is to open or close the doors fully. It is best to close the bedroom and closet doors while sleeping. But if you need the door open for safety or ventilation feel free to do so.

If the knob of one door can touch the knob of any other door, you have a situation known as "clashing knobs." The knobs symbolize heads butting and add a vibration of conflict or argument. If you live alone, you might assume there is usually no one around

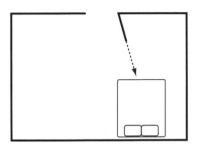

Poison arrow from door

to argue with. Well, you can always argue with yourself, and that means having a difficult time making up your mind. Sometimes it is possible to simply hang one door on the opposite side of the door frame. If that can be done, the situation is fixed completely. If that cannot be done, then learn to love red ribbons. Yes, they can look awkward in many homes, but they are a powerful feng shui tool.

Red Ribbons

Red symbolizes new blood, a fresh beginning. Just as with bamboo flutes, described on pages 29-30, the ribbon should be cut to nine inches or a multiple of nine inches, because it is the highest single-digit number and conveys strength into the intention. In this case, the intention is to reduce conflict. Tie the red ribbon to any knob that can touch any other knob. At least two knobs get ribbons. Items that can be used instead of ribbons are yarn, thick thread, or tassels. It does not matter how far down the ribbons actually hang once they are tied. At the moment of tying the ribbon, have your intention in mind, and say it out loud using whatever words feel appropriate.

MIRRORS

Mirrors have many purposes in feng shui. They expand a space and bring in fresh energy. They repel menacing objects and poison arrows, and they keep chi from quickly vanishing out a window. Mirrors also symbolically seal off one area from another, such as a bathroom from a bedroom. Mirrors can "bring back" a missing area if the floor plan of the room is not a perfect square or rectangle. See Chapter Ten, The Shape of the Bedroom. Another use of mirrors is to empower you when you have your back to the door.

Mirrors are quite controversial in bedrooms, especially mirrors that reflect the bed. Some feng shui teachers warn against them, citing such things as disturbed sleep and unfaithful relationships. Other teachers praise mirrors in bedrooms, saying they lessen tensions and improve relationships. My biggest concern with mirrors in bedrooms is how well does the person sleep? If there is a history of disturbed sleep, I recommend removing mirrors from the bedroom or covering them when sleeping. It can be tried as an experiment for a few months to see if sleep improves. If you have mirrors in the bedroom and sleep soundly, I doubt the mirrors are causing any problem. Instead, they could be bringing an expansiveness to your life.

Do not have a mirror in a Fortunate Blessings area (back left corner as seen from the bedroom door)—see page 94. A mirror represents a window. This is especially true when the mirror reflects the view from a window, as when the window is on a wall opposite or adjacent to the mirror. However, mirrors located anywhere in the room (even a mirrored tabletop) can represent a window. Windows of any kind are a "leak opportunity" for chi. That leak is mainly a problem when it occurs in a Fortunate Blessings area. The fewer windows in a Fortunate Blessings area, the better. The fewer mirrors in a Fortunate Blessings area, the better also.

A mirror is always okay in a bedroom when it is used to reflect the door, so that someone in bed can see the door. Of course, it is preferable not to arrange the furniture so as to create that kind of situation in the first place. But sometimes there is no other option. More information on using mirrors to see a doorway is on pages 24-25.

Mirrors indicate how truly and honestly you see yourself. They should always be clean and in good repair, no cracks, and no bad silvering. A cracked mirror gives you a fractured image of yourself, as do mirror tiles or any mirror that breaks up the image. Old mirrors with bad silvering cannot give you a true reflection of yourself, and may contribute to low self-esteem. If the mirror is an antique, the bad silvering actually adds to the value of the piece, and if that's the reason you own it, here's my suggestion. Have the old glass removed, save it, and replace it with new mirror glass. If and when you sell the piece, put the old mirror back in. The value is preserved, but you haven't had to live with the consequences of bad silvering for all those years. New mirror glass is not expensive. Avoid mirrors of smoked or colored glass. Some mirrors have designs etched or painted on them. It is best not to view yourself in such mirrors on a regular basis. If the design is just around the border, the mirror is probably okay.

If a mirror in the bedroom is used to see yourself, it should show all of your head. If all of the head cannot be seen, you may experience problems such as headaches or unclear thinking. Ideally, a mirror should also show the space eight inches above your head, because that represents your potential. A bedroom mirror's ideal shape is round or oval. Those shapes are more yin, whereas square or rectangular mirrors are more yang.

TELEVISIONS

If possible, do not have a television in the bedroom. If that isn't feasible, cover the television when not in use, or have it in a cabinet that can be closed. If you use the television to help you get sleepy and turn it off with the remote control, this can lead to disturbed and garbled dreams. There are other ways to promote sleep: read, meditate, reflect on the day, or chat with someone close to you. Use your imagination. Unless you are very rich, you are not going to have a device that raises or lowers the television so that it is out of sight with the push of a button. Here's the bottom line: If you get sound sleep with the screen uncovered, then it is probably not affecting you. Covering a television (or computer monitor) when not in use is a bold statement about priorities in your life. The priority of the bedroom must always be good, solid rest.

CLOCKS

Bedroom clocks should be silent—no loud ticking. They should show the time accurately (within a few minutes). A clock that does not show the correct time brings with it a vibration of untrustworthiness. If a clock is stuck and doesn't work, have it repaired or get rid of it. It is holding you back in the past.

Digital clocks that plug into a wall socket (such as clock radios) often have a surprisingly powerful electromagnetic field (EMF). The field can be measured to determine how far the clock should be from a sleeper's body. Meters for measuring EMFs are available from such manufacturers as AlphaLab (800-769-3754; www.trifield.com). The meters aren't cheap, and if you just want to be on the safe side, make sure any plug-in digital clock is several feet from your body. Especially, do not have the clock near your head.

BOOKS

It is fine to have a few books in the bedroom, just not too many. The bedroom should not resemble a library. Do not have a lot of books or magazines near the bed, such as on a bedside table. Two or three books is plenty there. Books contain words and thoughts, and are considered busy. If many books need to be kept in the bedroom, try to keep them out of sight—see page 58.

If hardback books are kept in view, consider removing the dust covers. Those dust covers help sell and protect the book when it is in a store. Once you own the book, remove the dust cover and allow the lovely cloth binding (nicely yin) with attractive lettering to be visible. The actual binding of a hardback is not only more elegant than the dust cover, it is also visually quieter. This is how the book is supposed to look in your home. It says that you own it. Do not discard the dust cover. It usually contains information about the author that is nowhere else in the book, and the dust cover is 90 percent of the book's resale value. If you're storing a lot of dust covers, I recommend filing them in alphabetical order by book title. However, if the books are in a sunny location, keep the dust covers on. Otherwise the book covers will fade.

DOLLS AND COLLECTIBLES

Dolls and plush animals are not appropriate in adult bedrooms on a regular basis. See page 125.

Any collection of collectibles would be better in a more yang room, such as a family room or living room. Collection refers to a large number of similar small decorative items that serve no purpose. Almost any collection possesses a busyness because of the quantity of the items, which are often quite detailed. Collectibles (except weapons) are fine in bedrooms—just not a whole collection of them.

LAMPS

Bedroom lamps can be simple or fancy but avoid using lamps that have sharp right angles, because they can cause poison arrows. Lamps, like nightstands, must not aim a poison arrow at a sleeper's body. See the illustration on page 56.

Fabric or paper shades are more yin than metal or plastic. Generally, they would be better for bedrooms. A relationship bed should preferably have matching lamps on each side. Bedroom lamp color should be muted, rather than vivid. Beyond that, one of the main color considerations should be related to the bagua area of the room. See Chapter Nine, the Bagua. Also, Chapter Eight has information on lighting in its many forms, not just lamps.

EXERCISE EQUIPMENT

Exercise equipment has a yang quality because its use is active. Even exercise equipment that is seldom used has this quality. Ideally, exercise equipment should not be kept in the bedroom, but we don't live in an ideal world, and sometimes there is no other option. Exercise equipment that is kept in the bedroom should be stored out of sight. A screen is perfect, but small bedrooms may not have enough room for one. It is okay just to drape nice fabric over the equipment. Preferably, don't store exercise equipment under the bed, especially if you are a light sleeper.

PLANTS

A moderate number of plants can be an energetic asset in the bedroom. The plants can be artificial or real. Artificial plants do not add the etheric vibrancy (and oxygen) of real plants, but do use them if they appeal to you and look appropriate. Artificial plants must be dusted—and washed—every so often to stay looking good. Run them under a shower. Cheap-looking plastic flowers are not preferred; it is better to use quality silk flowers.

Don't use dried plants as decoration in the bedroom unless they are changed at least twice a year. Dried plants are dead, and their energy reads dead. Live chi energy once flowed through them as sap. The sap is gone and they begin to rob you of your vitality and hold you back in the past. Some people like to keep dried flowers from sentimental occasions. It is truly not a good idea. Let them go back to the earth. Fresh energy with your name on it has been waiting for that moment. Artificial plants do not have this characteristic because sap never flowed through them. Potpourri is commonly used in bedrooms but is not recommended because the flowers are dead and are often scented with synthetic perfumes.

Spiky plants are almost never recommended in feng shui. Avoid any plant that you wouldn't feel comfortable going up to and shaking hands with. This is especially true in the bedroom.

Grow plants with rounded leaves in the bedroom. If there is a window box outside a bedroom window, the plants should also have rounded leaves.

Plants that are particularly appropriate in bedrooms are those with fuzzy leaves, such as:

- African violets, which bloom almost constantly.
- Purple velvet plant *(Gynura aurantiaca)*. This soft foliage plant is easy to grow, but can get leggy if not pinched back.
- Teddy-bear plant *(Cyanotis kewensis)*. This plant likes to trail down, but doesn't have an overabundance of drooping plants. They can bring a feeling of depression.
- *Kalanchoe.* There are several Kalanchoes with wonderfully fuzzy leaves: *tomentosa, beharensis,* and *belutina.*

Another delightful plant for the bedroom with a bright window is the Polkadot plant *(Hypoestes phyllostachya)*. Even when it is not blooming, it looks very attractive, with pink splashes on green leaves. It is a perfect plant for the relationship area of a bedroom, the far right corner—see pages 110-111.

FOUNTAINS

Fountains involve water, and water is yin when compared to dryness (which is yang). But there is very yang water (Niagara Falls) and very yin water (Okefenokee Swamp). A fountain is yang because it is active—probably too active for most bedrooms. Do not put a fountain near the head of the bed even if it is turned off at night. Fountains are always fine in guest rooms. In a guest room their activity is welcome, since the room is too yin, because it is used infrequently. Allow the fountain to flow all the time if it will not irritate anyone. Fountains work best if run constantly. It does require a commitment to replenish the water regularly because of evaporation. Distilled water will prolong the life of the motor. If possible, place the fountain in the Fortunate Blessings corner. When guests are staying in the room, show them how to turn the fountain off at night.

Fountains are often appropriate in a studio apartment, but they should be turned off when someone is sleeping. See page 132.

Fountains are also good for masking noise. I'd take a good fountain over a noise machine any time.

Plants, cats, and birds love fountains. It makes their environment more natural. Cats appreciate drinking the moving water, and birds love them for bathing.

Fountains that have a light bulb in the water (or very close to the water) represent conflict. This is because the elements Fire and Water are conflicting elements. See page 94. A spotlight shining on the rippling water is fine because it is not in close physical proximity to the water.

For the same reason, a fountain with a fogging machine is not recommended. The fog is caused by intense heat.

Be sure the pump motor noise is very quiet. Silence is ideal. In the quiet of your own home, any motor noise is more noticeable than it is in a store. In the store, put your ear right next to the motor while it is running. If it sounds noisy there, it will sound a lot noisier in your home.

Make sure the oversplash is well contained in the catching basin. The motor should be turned up fairly high to have lots of splash sound, but if there is oversplash on wood furniture, its surface will be damaged. Make sure there is no oversplash or that the fountain is on a hard surface like marble.

A fountain should not aim a single stream of water into a basin. That's a bathroom sound. A babbling-brook sound is quite different. It is caused by many drops splashing on different levels.

ALTARS

It is fine to have an altar or shrine in the bedroom, especially if you want one and there is no other appropriate spot in the home. A bedroom altar should be simple. The simpler the better, generally speaking. If possible, the altar should be at heart level or higher. Try not to place the altar directly opposite the foot of the bed. Such a position means your feet are pointing toward the sacred image, and that is considered disrespectful.

Feng shui doesn't care whether or not you have an altar. However, in the unlikely event that your bedroom window opens out to a cemetery, you should do something to counter its effect. Consider keeping a small light on an image that you feel is sacred or protective.

PICTURES

If the bedroom is used just for sleeping, do not hang too many pictures. The ideal might be one per wall, with some walls having none. If your decorating sense tells you to put up more pictures, then do so, but not to excess.

Pictures behind glass are okay in bedrooms, but if it is feasible, try to have some of the pictures not behind glass. Glass is hard and slick and thereby quite yang. Nonglare glass is more yin than regular glass. It diffuses reflected light and brings a pleasant softness to the bedroom. Nonglare glass works best if it directly touches the picture. It is also fine to have one layer of matte, but multiple layers make the artwork less distinct.

To use feng shui principles in selecting the imagery of the bedroom pictures, see page 94. Don't use pictures (or sculpture) with missing body parts (such as the Venus de Milo) unless the artwork is a bust or a head portrait. Something like a bust of Nefertiti is fine because it was intended as a bust (i.e., nothing got broken off). If a picture shows most of a body, but not the head, it probably should not be on display. Also don't display pictures of ruins. They say that your glory years are a thing of the past.

The view from the bed is important because it is what you wake up to. It represents the future. You should like the view at the foot of the bed. Sometimes the view is just closet doors. Oh, well, just keep them clean. If the view at the foot of the bed is a blank wall, consider putting a picture there that you truly love. If the bed is a relationship bed, both people should love the picture equally—no compromise.

RUGS AND CARPETS

Feng shui approves of wall-to-wall carpet in bedrooms if it works in your situation. It absorbs sound, especially with a pad under it. It also adds a yin softness that helps the restful purpose of the room. It is fine to put beautiful rugs, such as sculpted Chinese rugs, over plain carpet. But the rugs must not slip. A rug over a carpet can tend to slide around. In that case use a special pad that grips both, and holds the rug in place. The pad is available at rug stores and some hardware stores. A rug over plain carpet is fine, but a rug over another rug is not fine. It is too busy and chaotic.

If there is bare floor in the bedroom, at least have a bedside rug. Have one on each side of the bed if two people sleep there. If the rugs slip (at all) use nonskid pads under them. Rugs that slip say that you do not have a steady foundation. Round or oval rugs are preferred for bedrooms because of their yin quality.

UNDER THE BED

Ideally, the area under the bed should be empty and unseen. The bed should not appear to be floating in space. With a bed skirt (or a platform bed) the bed becomes more connected to the earth, and more grounded. That groundedness will be conveyed to the sleeper.

Having the area around the bed empty is not practical for everyone. If things must be stored under the bed, always use appropriate boxes or drawers. They help seal away the objects.

Store soft things, such as fabric, not hard things such as tools. Clean bedding can be stored under the bed as long as it is in boxes or drawers. Don't store things that require active or thoughtful use, no exercise equipment, and no paper with words on it, including books. Also, don't store shoes unless they are organized in boxes with lids.

SMELL

How a room or dwelling smells is very important. Smell can be considered an object because what is being inhaled are tiny particles of something. Needless to say, that something should be pleasant in the bedroom (and hopefully in all rooms). If there is a good fresh-air smell already present, I would leave it alone. Fresh air is ideal.

If it seems good to add fragrance to a bedroom, aromatherapy has a lot to offer. Aromatherapy is a kindred art to feng shui. It is a recent name for an ancient art that has been studied by many cultures. Diffusing essential oils is the recommended technique in aromatherapy books, as well as the use of scented candles or potpourri. Incense is also commonly used by those who don't mind the smoke. Fragrant plants in and around the bedroom are a special delight. The fragrances aromatherapy associates with relaxation are: lavender, rose, patchouli, jasmine, chamomile, narcissus, frangipani (Plumeria), cypress, clary sage, and neroli.

SOUND

Sound is not precisely an object, but it sure is tangible. Less is better when it comes to restful sleep. The only time sound is beneficial to sleep is when it masks a more disturbing sound. A fountain is sometimes a suitable remedy for obnoxious traffic and sidewalk noise, but do not add sound to an already quiet bedroom when sleeping.

When no one is asleep in the bedroom, you can use sound. A fountain on a timer is sometimes a happy addition to a bedroom, especially in a studio apartment. Make sure the fountain is turned off when someone is sleeping. If televisions can be kept out of the bedroom, they should be. Their sound is considerably more yang than the sound of most radio. The sound of an action movie leaves a residual yang energy. On the opposite end of the spectrum, a stereo playing soft music is very yin and very appropriate for a bedroom.

If more than one person sleeps in the bedroom, and one of those people snores, it can be quite disturbing. A product called Snoreless, (www.snoreless.org) is reported to be very effective.

CLUTTER

If clutter seems to be a major challenge, I recommend Stephanie Winston's audiotape *Getting Organized* (see Recommended Reading). Audiotapes are a great way for busy people to continue to learn. You can listen to them while bathing or driving or at other times. After you play an audiotape a half-dozen times, you do start to get the message.

The number one rule of clutter (especially paper clutter) is stop bringing it home. You control most of the paper clutter that enters your home. Be ruthless. Even if it means canceling the newspaper—don't bring more paper into your home! Some of the most helpful tips are in Jeff Campbell's *Clutter Control*. (See Recommended Reading, page 157.)

The number two rule is to make an appointment with yourself (daily if possible) to clear the clutter and get more organized. Two habits—television watching and magazine/newspaper reading—often eat up a person's time and attention and can cause indefinite postponement of clutter clearing. The television viewing should be less important than the clutter clearing. If you are a television watcher and you have any kind of clutter problem, turn off the television and leave it off until you become a well-organized, on-top-of-it person. It won't kill you to stop watching television so that you can do something more important: clear the clutter.

I do believe that the energetic effects of clutter can be devastating to your body and spirit. Being well organized will improve your life in more ways than you can imagine. I am not overstating it to say that having a good sense of structure about your daily life is a great aid to accomplishing the true purpose of your life.

No one should structure their daily life around watching certain programs at certain times. Use a VCR that easily records those must-see programs to watch without commercials.

If you watch a lot of television, please reclaim your life. There is great purpose and potential in every person's life. It is doubtful that watching television is an expression of that purpose. Everyone has a mental "to do" list. It is powerful to write down your list. It is even more powerful to check off the items when they were accomplished. Use the time you've saved by not watching television (or reading magazines) to get organized and accomplish your greatest goals. Use feng shui and get there faster.

Where do you start the process of removing the clutter? Begin at the door of the room, and expand out to a three or four foot radius of clutter-free zone. Chi energy should pour freshly into your bedroom through the doorway. Clutter that is very close to the doorway has an immediate stagnating effect on that fresh chi. The subliminal message of the clutter is, "Do this—do that!" The chi energy picks up that message and falls flat on its face. Clear the doorway area so that fresh, enriching chi can flow into your bedroom. It will consequently flow into your life.

The other place to begin is in your Fortunate Blessings corner. Yes, there are two places to begin. Consider both of them to be equally important. Other names for the Fortunate Blessings area are Intention and Empowerment. If it is your intention to live a clutter-free life, the message rings powerfully from this area into the rest of the room. It acts as a psychic gong, ringing in the new clutter-free vibration.

Do not allow clutter to be reflected in a mirror—it is then symbolically doubled and made more daunting. If things are cluttering up your life but you can't bring yourself to part with them, remember this rule: the more things you have, the less time you have. It is so true. If you aren't actively using an object or love it dearly, you may want to part with it, even if it was a gift.

CHAPTER EIGHT

Lighting

The quality of light greatly influences the energy of the bedroom. Interior design acknowledges five kinds of lighting. (See *Lighting Style* in Recommended Reading.)

Ambient light is the main light (usually overhead). It is the light you would use when cleaning the room. Windows often provide the main ambient light during the day.

Task light is used for specific tasks. A lamp on a bedside table provides light for reading. Lighting around a mirror illuminates your face.

Accent light provides visual interest in a room. A spotlight aimed at artwork accents the piece. A spotlight on the floor behind a plant and aimed up is a fine way to use accent light.

Decorative light refers to a light fixture that is decorative, such as a chandelier or a beautiful stained-glass night light.

Kinetic light is light that moves. This refers to anything from a fireplace or a candle, to a television or computer screen.

Each type of lighting has specific feng shui concerns.

AMBIENT LIGHTING

The ambient light should provide adequate light so that you can do a good job of cleaning the room. The room should not be so dim it feels depressive. At least during the day, the room should be bright. However, a bedroom can be too bright, for example, by having too many windows. Windows are a wonderful source of light and fresh air, but direct sunlight pouring into a window is very yang. Many large windows and glass doors hinder the restful yin energy. Windows yes, but not too many. Floor-to-ceiling glass in bedrooms is definitely not recommended. If there are too many windows, use drapes (or other heavy and soft window treatment) at night. If a bedroom has many sunlit windows that remain uncovered during the day, it may not be truly restful at night. The residue of the bright yang remains in the room. It might be best to cover some of them during the day—if only with sheers.

The ambient light at night is often a combination of several types of lighting. A bedside lamp (task) and a corner uplight (accent) can provide adequate, subdued ambient light for this yin room. If the bedroom is multifunctional, the lighting should be adjusted to the room's current use. When a desk light (task) is turned off, it signals that the desk energy (active, thinking—yang) is not present. When only candles are burning (kinetic, but very yin), it signals that peace and quiet are predominant.

Ideally, the ambient light should be easy to adjust. This is often as easy as installing a dimmer in the light switch for the overhead light. The room can be bright for cleaning or trying on clothes, and dimmer for a quiet time before sleep. Be sure the dimmer does not cause the light bulb to hum or buzz. Not all dimmers are created equal.

If the bedroom has an overhead light in the center of the room, note the shape of the finial. The finial is the metal tip that holds the glass shade in place. The finial should be well-rounded. A sharply pointed finial can direct a poison arrow into the center of the room. This is especially troublesome if the bed is directly under the light fixture. Blunt or rounded finials are available at hardware stores and at lighting supply stores. Only the finial needs to be changed, not the whole fixture.

TASK LIGHTING

A bedside lamp is the most obvious bedroom task light. Its task is to provide light for reading in bed, perhaps the most common presleep activity. When the bedside light is on, it is an energetic pull to come to bed. Other possible task lights in a bedroom might be a lamp by a reading chair or a desk lamp. A combination of task lights can make a softer ambient light than a stark overhead light. A desk lamp is the one task light that I suggest turning off when the task is finished. As long as the desk lamp is on, it causes an energetic pull to the desk and its yang busyness.

ACCENT LIGHTING

An accent light does not have to shine on an object per se. It can just be a splash of light along a surface of the room. If the room is painted a rich, saturated color, an accent light can let its beauty be appreciated more at night.

A can light behind plants is an easy way to bring accent lighting into the bedroom. The pot of the plant can hide the light and the ceiling and wall get great plant shadows. If you don't have a green thumb, you can use good artificial plants. This can bring fresh chi into what may have previously been a dark, dreary corner. More information on can lights is on page 20.

DECORATIVE LIGHTING

Decorative lighting can be a bit on the yang side. It says, "notice me." A decorative light is any light that is distinctive and lovely enough to stand on its own as a decorative object. A crystal chandelier or a stained glass shade (such as a turtle light or a seashell light) are examples of decorative lighting. A chandelier is rarely appropriate in a bedroom. It has an unmistakable "look at me" quality that pulls chi energy up and makes it more yang.

An exception would be a chandelier of candles, which have a romantic yin quality. Other decorative lights are unmistakably yin. These include night lights and any variety of cute small lights illuminating lovely colored glass or plastic. Often the shape is beautiful, such as a turtle with a glass shell and a small bulb inside. Such lighting is yin because of its subtlety. It is good to put decorative lights on a quiet timer so that you don't have to think about turning them on. They come on in the evening and they go off at bedtime (as a good reminder).

Here is an example of decorative lighting in an unusual bedroom situation. Jill was having trouble with her teenage daughter. It didn't take a psychic to feel the lousy vibes in her bedroom. The biggest reason was that the only bedroom window was exactly on the property line, and the neighbor's wall was about four inches away on the other side of the glass. The window got no light. It was a window onto "perpetual night." The solution was to hang strands of tiny, clear holiday lights on the outside of the window. Even better would have been tiny lights that could slowly blink.

If you like the idea of tiny, clear lights, feel free to use them in various ways in the bedroom. They are unmistakably romantic. If they are kept on a quiet timer, they are easier to enjoy. Changing the settings on the timer to match the seasonal light changes connects us to the natural cycle of the earth's rotation.

Also, those tiny lights clicking off is a very sweet reminder to go to bed.

KINETIC LIGHTING

The ideal kinetic bedroom light is natural—candles or a fireplace. However, they are not possible, appropriate, or even desirable in many instances. Candles must be used with the same awareness as a stove burner that is turned on. Candles could conceivably burn down the house. They probably won't, and they usually don't, but do be careful. Do not burn candles near curtains. Be wary of using wooden candlesticks unless there is a metal insert that fits around the candle base. If you use candles for decoration in your bedroom, be sure you place them where they won't cause trouble. Candles with wooden shelves a few inches above them are dangerous.

Eight-hour votive candles are one of the safest kinds of candles. So you don't break their glass holder, burn the candle fully at one time. If the candle is extinguished then re-lit, the glass heats too quickly and is likely to crack when the wax is almost gone. The votive candle holder can be the correct color for the bagua area in the room. (See the next chapter.) A candle that burns in a glass container can cause black soot on the inside of the glass. Keep the black soot wiped off between burnings. Thick candles burn down the center, leaving a wall of wax surrounding the flame. Use a knife to trim the wall of wax level with the bottom of the black part of the wick. The trimming is best done soon after the candle has been extinguished. The wax is soft, and it is easy to remove the excess wax down to a smooth, level surface. Such a candle, when it is relit, will be brighter. Do not display candles with an unburned wick. Unused candles count as clutter. Burning the wick, if only once, says the candles are of use. Ideally, candles should be made of a natural material such as beeswax, should not be scented with synthetic perfumes, and should not have a lead core in the wick.

Fireplaces can provide romantic kinetic light even without a roaring log fire. Gas fireplaces make a gentle, kinetic light that is appreciated any night. If the fireplace is not plumbed for gas, it is almost always safe to insert a blazing collection of candles into the fireplace. A blazing collection of candles is usually quite safe in a fireplace. Such kinetic lighting transforms the bedroom.

If real fire is not feasible or appropriate, a very low-watt flicker bulb behind a translucent screen can be kinetic and decorative at the same time. It can gently light up a part of the room that felt dark and stagnant beforehand.

Any other form of electrically generated kinetic light in the bedroom is most likely coming from a television or a computer screen. Neither is preferred in the bedroom according to feng shui. If they must be in the bedroom, do not keep them on unnecessarily or used as background lighting.

When dealing with kinetic lights, keep the motion slow and gentle. That makes the lighting more yin and more restful for a bedroom.

CHAPTER NINE

The Bagua

The bagua (or pakua) is a grid that overlays the floor plan of the bedroom. There are nine areas in the room—eight around the walls, and one in the center. These areas relate to aspects of a person's life. The bagua is largely based on the eight *I Ching* trigrams (see Glossary if you are not familiar with the *I Ching*) which identify with the eight areas, or guas, around the center. It is also based on the Five Elements. The areas that most strongly relate to a particular element are the five areas that are not in corners. See the illustration on the following page.

A bagua grid can be laid over a room, or over the house as a whole, based on the front door as the entrance. It is most powerful when applied per room, because when you are in a room, that's the space that is affecting you the most at that time—not some distant part of the home. It can also be applied to a parcel of land, usually based on the driveway entrance. It can even be applied to a desktop.

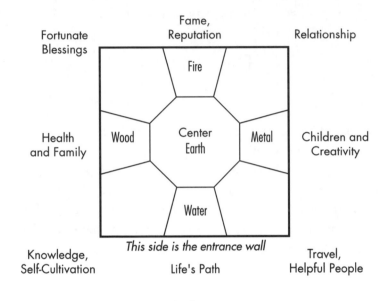

Fortunate Blessings

Fame, Reputation

Relationship

Health and Family

Wood

Center Earth

Metal

Children and Creativity

Fire

Water

This side is the entrance wall

Knowledge, Self-Cultivation

Life's Path

Travel, Helpful People

The bagua

THE FIVE ELEMENTS

According to Taoist teaching, all the manifest energy of the universe can be divided among five archetypal elements—Water, Wood, Fire, Metal, and Earth. Shapes and colors signify each individual element.

Water—The shape is wavy or free-form like waves, or a river meandering, or a drop that's splashed. The color is black like a deep, dark well.

Wood—The shape is square or a vertical rectangle like tree trunks. The color is green like leaves; blue works equally well.

Fire—The shape is any angular shape like a pyramid or cone, symbolizing a flame rising. The color is red.

Metal—The shape is round, oval, or arched. The color is white. Imagine light glinting off polished metal. That glint is taken to be white. This also includes very light colors such as pastels.

Earth—The shape is square or a horizontal rectangle symbolizing the horizon. The color is yellow or any earth tone such as brown or burnt orange.

Before explaining the nine bagua areas in detail, one more feng shui concept should be explained—the concept of Elemental Cycles. At this point, feng shui can take a major detour into the world of the complicated. The background of knowledge of the elemental cycles can put off some people, but it is a great aid in feng shui. It is particularly useful in working with the individual bagua areas. For instance, if it were desirable to enhance the Fame area, but red colors and fiery symbols were inappropriate for the decor, wood items could be used because wood feeds fire.

ELEMENTAL CYCLES

The five elements relate to each other in several dynamic cycles of creation and destruction. The study of these cycles can be daunting to a beginner, and for simplicity I am only including the standard creation and destruction cycles.

In the *creative cycle* each element is considered to give birth to the next element.

> Wood creates Fire (Wood is the fuel)
> Fire creates Earth (ashes are as dirt)
> Earth creates Metal (through time and pressure)
> Metal creates Water (through condensation)
> Water creates Wood (Water is essential to plants)

The *destructive cycle* is not the reverse of the creative cycle. The interaction is rearranged, and the result is quite negative.

> Wood destroys Earth (plants eat dirt)
> Earth destroys Water (the result is mud)
> Water destroys Fire (quite obviously)
> Fire destroys Metal (through melting)
> Metal destroys Wood (axes and saws kill trees)

These cycles can be called upon in deciding what to do when there is too much of an element in the room.

When there is too much:	Add:
Wood	Fire or Metal
Water	Fire or Earth
Metal	Fire or Wood
Earth	Wood or Water
Fire	Earth or Water

APPLYING THE BAGUA

To apply the bagua, imagine it enlarged and stretched to fit the bedroom. An example of how a bagua is shaped for a rectangular bedroom is shown in the illustration below.

There are two equally popular approaches to orienting the bagua. In one approach the door to the room is the key orienting factor. The door is known as the "mouth of chi." We enter

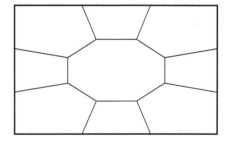

Rectangular bagua

through the door, and so does chi. This method of orienting the bagua places the grid so the side that says Water is along the entrance wall. Several schools of feng shui use the entrance to orient the bagua. Some of them are: Eight-point, Black Sect, Intuitive, and Pyramid. None of those names says much about it, so I generally refer to it as "entrance-based bagua" for the sake of clarity.

The other method of orienting the bagua is based on the cardinal directions—north, south, east, west. This type of feng shui relies heavily on Chinese astrology and numerology, and is called Compass School. To use this method, place the side of the grid that says Fire to the south.

People who have read more than one book about feng shui sometimes become quite confused. They may have read different approaches to orienting the bagua. Most books fail to mention that there is more than one way to do it. Pick one method of orienting the bagua. Use the entrance or use the compass. Stick with that method or give it a good try for at least six months. If you mix and match the two different methods of orienting the bagua, you will not be practicing good feng shui, guaranteed.

This book bases the bagua on the entrance. I have nothing against numerology or astrology. I'm sure they are fine systems, but I do not base my life on them, nor do I not ask my clients to do so. I am more drawn to arranging furniture and household items beautifully and correctly. If you want Chinese astrology and numerology to play a more active role in your life, orient the bagua with the Fame area to the south. You should also read a good book on Compass School feng shui, such as *Practical Feng Shui* by Simon Brown. (See Recommended Reading.)

What follows is a list of the nine guas (or bagua areas) with suggestions for improving or enhancing them.

Life's Path

Water is the element in the center of the entrance wall of the room. It symbolizes movement and has to do with one's journey through life. It is often referred to as the Career area, but it relates to more than just income-earning livelihood. When water is moving it is responding to a natural law—gravity. It is very powerful to put a picture of flowing water in this area, a picture of a stream, river, or gentle waterfall. A major waterfall such as Niagara or Victoria Falls is a bit too powerful. If such a picture were in the Life's Path area it would be like asking for a stampede in your life. It is not ideal to put a picture of still or stagnant water here, such as a lake, pond, or the ocean. The ocean is not considered to be going anywhere—just moving back and forth. By representing flowing water in the Life's Path area, you are setting up a dynamic in your own life to keep yourself on track with your life's purpose.

Black is the ideal color in this area, but if that just isn't you, use whatever dark tones appeal to you. Even dark furniture will do. Items made of glass are good to use here, especially if they have a free-form, watery look. In fact, any free-form, amorphous objects are appropriate here. Mirrors also represent water. Water features such as a fountain are a possibility, keeping in mind the cautions about fountains in bedrooms on page 74.

If you are undergoing a career change, be sure this area stays clutter-free to allow fresh energy to flow in easily. Items that have to do with your career are appropriate in this area.

Knowledge and Self-Cultivation

Wisdom, Meditation, and Contemplation are other names for this area. The *I Ching* trigram for this area is Mountain; it is a great place to put pictures of mountains, representing a mountain of knowledge. It is also a good place for images of deities, spiritual teachers, and wise people. It is an excellent area for an altar. It would be best to leave out images of water because the element that is often associated with this area is Earth. When earth and water mix, the result is mud. Black, blue, and green are the ideal colors, but the blue and green should preferably be dark tones.

Books, stereos, and other learning tools are appropriate here, including televisions and computers. Such things are questionable in a bedroom, but sometimes there is no other place for them in the home.

Health and Family

The family that this area refers to is your ancestors—your parents and those who came before them. If you want pictures of those people in your bedroom (many people don't), put them in this area. They are able to offer more resonance in your life from this gua. It's appropriate that this area also represents health because our genes can predispose us to certain health conditions or immunities.

Wood is the element here and plants are perfect in the Health/Family area, especially trees such as ficus or palms. Representations of plants are also good—any pictures of healthy growing plants, especially trees. Wooden furniture is ideal here. Metal furniture is not so ideal, metal implements being a major destroyer of living trees. Items that represent fire such as candles, angular objects, red things, and fireplaces should not be in this area, or they should be kept to a minimum here. If there is a fireplace in this area it can portend health problems such as fatigue. De-emphasize the fireplace by using an opaque screen. Items that represent Water or Earth are good in this area because that's what plants need to grow.

The shape for Wood is rectangular, like tall growing trees. Square is also good. Tall, wooden furniture (such as shelving, a cabinet, or an armoire) is perfect to use in this area. The best colors are green and/or blue.

Fortunate Blessings

This area is commonly called the Wealth Corner for good reason. It represents prosperity in its many forms, including, of course, money. Other names for this area are Intention and Empowerment. It is a powerful area, and improvements here are like waving a red flag to the Universe.

One basic thing to know about this area is that it must be clean, uncluttered, and well-maintained. If anything in this area is broken, either fix it or move it. If anything in this area is useless, get rid of it. It is great to have plants here (the bigger the better), but they must be healthy, look vibrant, and have no thorns or sharp pointy leaves.

As you might imagine, the Wealth area is an ideal place to put expensive things—things that were a stretch for you to afford. Paying more than you had budgeted for an object in the Fortunate Blessings area gives you what I call "the ouch factor." It hurt your pocketbook. The symbolism of it being an expensive object is present in your life. The money you spent for it will come back to you many times over.

Royal purple is an ideal color here, as well as cobalt blue, and bold Chinese red. Green can also be a good color here because Wood is the element that is often associated with this area. Gold also works because it indicates wealth and represents Earth, which feeds Wood. Use rich, vibrant, saturated colors, and if the colors are appropriately brilliant, you don't always have to use a lot to be effective. You probably shouldn't try to use all the colors here. The result would probably be quite a hodgepodge. This area should look nice (if not gorgeous).

Fountains are absolutely perfect in this area. But because it's a bedroom, see the cautions on page 75. Prismatic crystals are great here and so are wind chimes. Mirrors are not great here because they represent windows and they are an opportunity for chi to leak away. Trash cans should not be in this corner of the room. That says that you are throwing your money away. If, for some reason, the trash must be in this corner, the can should have a lid so chi energy doesn't find it. One client commented, "It's pretty easy to fool chi energy."

Fame

This area has to do with your reputation and the future, and with what people are saying about you. Fire is the element here, and it is represented by red, ideally a brilliant primary red. Such a saturated color is not always appropriate to add to a bedroom. However, if you need fame in your work, I advise you to learn to love this color. Thousands of dollars of publicity will not buy what the bold use of candy-apple red can achieve if used in the Fame area. If you need fame, you cannot overdo it. If you just want a good reputation, you certainly can tone it down. Maroon, old rose, magenta, basically any color that is in the warm end of the spectrum will have a good effect. Dusty rose is often the best choice for a bedroom. If it is a relationship bedroom, the warm color will say that there is a warm relationship.

The shape for Fire is pointed, like a flame rising up. Cones, pyramids and triangles are appropriate, as well as any shape that is sharply angular. Examples are red tapered candles or a picture of buildings with red, pointed roofs. Fireplaces are auspicious in this area. It is the one area where I most definitely do not recommend water features (such as fountains) or representations of water (such as ocean pictures.) This area is perfect for hanging diplomas or awards, especially with red frames or red matting.

Animals are considered to have the spark of life within them, so items of animal origin are appropriate here. Such things might be made of leather, feathers, bone, horn, or fur. Pictures or figurines of animals are also good. Avoid things that come from or represent water animals in this area, such as seashells or sand dollars or pictures of fish or sea mammals.

Relationship

The Relationship area doesn't just concern romantic relationships. It concerns relationships of all kinds, friends, co-workers, et cetera. The most important thing to note about this area is that there should not be any outstanding single object here. If there is a pole lamp, it should be supported by more than one pole or have more than one bulb. It is best if things in this area relate to each other. There is a design concept that things are either in conflict or in conversation. In this area, they need to be in conversation. As for pictures, it would be best if they were in pairs or groupings. If there is only one picture, it should have several items within it, such as a group of flowers, or a couple of people. This is an ideal place to put a grouping of almost anything. However, things that might represent conflict, such as guns or swords, should never be kept in the Relationship area or anywhere on display in a bedroom.

If a desk is in a Relationship area, certain desk items should not be on display. Anything that could conceivably cut or hurt someone should be stored out of sight. Put scissors in a drawer, and also put away the stapler, staple remover, tape dispenser, and letter opener. If the desk is not in the Relationship area of the room, it doesn't matter if those items are on view.

Be careful about the cutting items. They shouldn't be in the far right corner of any desk, no matter where it is in the room. That is the relationship area of the desk. More information on applying the bagua to a desk is on page 131.

This area especially concerns women and feminine energy. Pink is the ideal color here. Red, white, and yellow also work. Dusty rose counts as pink, and goes well in many decors. Avoid fabric with stripes (considered to represent conflict) in this area.

Things that have a romantic association are appropriate here—hearts and flowers, if that's your style. Televisions are not so appropriate. They can signify a life in which the television is the main relationship. If there is no other place to have the television, it is best to cover it when it is not in use. It is also good to have something higher than the television, such as pictures, above it on the wall. Higher says "more important." Telephones are fine in the Relationship area, and so are computers. Computers are used for two-way communication. Televisions are not.

Children and Creativity

If you have children, this area will always affect them, even if they have moved away. It will also affect your grandchildren and beyond. This is a great place to put pictures or mementos of your children or grandchildren. If you don't have children, this area is about your ideas and creativity. They are what you leave behind when you die. Metal is the element here and is represented by white or pastels. Objects that have a metallic finish are also appropriate. The shape for Metal is round, with oval or arched shapes being equally good. Creativity is associated with this element, and the rounded shapes help ideas flow. Some objects that would be very appropriate here are: round mirrors, round baskets, pictures with round matting or frames, round metal plates or trays, and round metal lamps or pole lights.

Helpful People and Travel

Heaven is the *I Ching* trigram for this area. People who help you can be thought of as heaven sent. This area of the room is a great place to put pictures of people who have been helpful to you, such as mentors, teachers, and benefactors—although not necessarily relatives. Images of deities or holy people would also be appropriate here, as well as angels or guardian beings.

If you would like to travel more, put a picture here of some-place far away, perhaps a picture of a place you've been or where you'd like to visit. Also any items that have come from other lands would be good here. Choose items that are obviously from far away.

This is an area for neutral tones , white, black, or gray. This area especially affects men and masculine energy.

Center

This area concerns health, and your ability to integrate all of who you are into a healthy personality. It is the only gua that touches all the other guas. Earth is represented by yellow or any earth tones such as ochre or brown. The shape is square or a horizontal rectangle. Pottery and beautiful sand are ways to bring real earth into this area. Representations of water are not recommended in the Center because the element is Earth, and when water and earth are mixed, the result is mud.

In ancient China (and many other cultures), the center of a house was often an open-air courtyard. Here one walked across actual earth to reach the various areas of the house. The healthi-est living spaces I have seen are those in which the center (of the room, house, or apartment) is open and uncluttered. This is hardly feasible in a small bedroom where the bed takes up most of the space. In that case, just try to have Earth represented by color or shape – for example a brown or yellow blanket at the foot of the bed.

Area (gua)	Alternate Name	Element	Color	Shape
Life's Path	Career, The Journey, Flow	Water	Black and very dark colors	Freeform, amorphous
Knowledge	Contemplation, Wisdom, Intuition, Meditation	Earth	Black, dark green, and dark blue	—
Health and Family	Ancestors, Elders, Community, New Beginnings	Wood	Green and blue	Vertical rectangle or square
Fortunate Blessings	Wealth, Intention, Empowerment, Abundance	Wood	Rich shades of purple, blue, red, and green	—
Fame	Reputation, Illumination, Future, Recognition	Fire	Red	Angular, pointed, triangular, conical, uprising
Relationship	Love, Marriage, Partnership, Commitment	Earth	Pink, white, red, and yellow	—
Children and Creativity	Descendants, Completion, Joy, Pleasure	Metal	White and pastels	Circular, oval, or arched
Helpful People and Travel	Benefactors, Compassion, Friends, Persistence	Metal	Black, white, or gray	—
Center	Health, Unity, Tai Chi, Wholeness	Earth	Yellow and earth tones such as brown, gold, and orange	Horizontal rectangle, square, or octagonal

I Ching Trigram	Meaning of Trigram	Comments
	Water	Perfect place for a fountain or a picture of flowing water.
	Mountain	Good place for books and learning tools, including television or computer.
	Thunder	Good place for plants and images of plants. Wooden furniture, especially tall.
	Wind	Expensive items, things that move or shimmer. No open trashcans. Perfect place for fountain or picture of water.
	Fire	Items related to fame—awards, diplomas. Things representing animals or made of animal—fur, bone, leather, feathers, etc.
	Earth	Pictures of loved ones, pairs and groupings of things. No outstanding singular objects. Preferably no television.
	Lake	Items that relate to children and/or creativity. If you have kids, the maintenance of this area will affect them.
	Heaven	Images of deities, angels, holy people, teachers, and mentors—also affirmations.
No trigram	—	No bathroom ever! A good place for keeping pottery. Try to keep this area open and transversable.

CHAPTER TEN

The Shape of the Bedroom

Most bedrooms are rectangular or square with flat ceilings. Great! Feng shui loves that. If this is what you have, you can skip this chapter. But if the floor plan of the bedroom is not a perfect square or rectangle, please read on.

EXTENSIONS AND MISSING AREAS

Any deviation from a perfect square or rectangle should be thought of as either an extension or a missing area. Extensions such as bay windows are generally to your benefit, but missing areas present a problem. They indicate a "lack" in that bagua area.

There are several methods for determining whether an irregular room has an extension or a missing area. Sometimes it is obvious by simply looking. The lengths of the pieces of the broken wall (made up of walls A and B in the first two illustrations) are compared. If the part of the wall that is farthest from the heart of the room (wall A in the missing area illustration) is longer, then there is a missing area outside the room. The gray areas in Illustrations 1

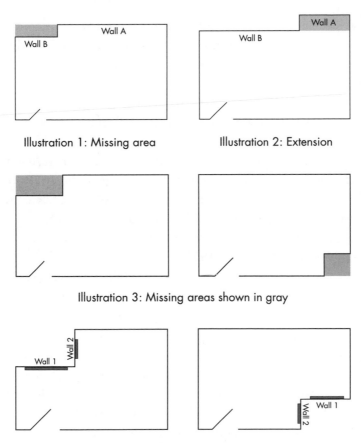

Illustration 1: Missing area

Illustration 2: Extension

Illustration 3: Missing areas shown in gray

Illustration 4: Locations of mirrors to bring back a missing area

113

and 3 are missing areas. If the wall that is farthest from the heart of the room (wall A in Illustration 2) is shorter than wall B, then there is an extension, with wall A as the outermost wall of the extension.

There are other methods for mathematically figuring whether rooms have missing areas or extensions. Different teachers usually have a particular method they prefer. Use the method that feels right to you. Use your intuition, experience, and a keen eye, noting such things as does the floor or ceiling change in the vicinity of the missing area or extension? Such a change often signals an extension. Anything that says "add-on" is usually an extension.

BRINGING BACK A MISSING AREA

If an area is missing from a room, it needs to be brought back. Do so by placing a mirror on wall one and wall two as indicated in Illustration 4. The mirrors should face into the bedroom. When bringing back a missing area, the mirror (or mirrors) should be as large as possible. This can present a problem in bedrooms, where many people prefer to keep mirrors to a minimum. If you prefer to keep mirrors to a minimum in the bedroom, but need to bring back a missing area, then consider placing the mirrors high on the wall, above head height. This is not appropriate in all decors. If it works in your decor, it will work even better if the mirror reflects something interesting or lovely. If it reflects something that is attention getting, it will be more effective because the interesting object will be reflected twice, and one of those reflections will appear to be inside the missing area. If you don't mind an excess of mirrors in the bedroom (see page 66) feel free to mirror walls one and two completely, but no mirror tiles. The visual effect is that the room actually extends into a corner. This causes the room to seem more like a square or rectangle.

You do not have to use that much mirror to be effective—it just won't be as effective. You can simply place a reasonably-sized mirror (larger than your head) on wall one or wall two. It does not have to be on both walls, and it does not have to be a large mirror. It will still be at least 80 percent effective at bringing back the missing area. The mirror serves as a window into another room. If you were Alice (as in *Alice Through the Looking Glass*) you could actually go into that room. You would still be in the same bedroom, because that is what the mirror is showing.

Mirrors are the most common way of bringing back a missing area, but if there is a window on wall one or wall two (of Illustration 4) perhaps it would work to have a window box just outside the window. A silent wind catcher placed outside the window is

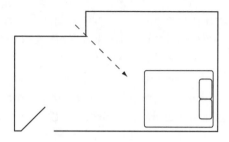

Illustration 5: Poison arrow caused by a corner

also helpful. You are thereby claiming occupancy of the missing area by using some of it.

An irregularly shaped bedroom often has a poison arrow that originates from a corner that juts into the room. If the poison arrow goes across the bed, as in Illustration 5, something must be done. If you own the home, I suggest you bullnose (see Glossary) the corner and forget about it. A rounded corner does not cause a poison arrow. If that isn't feasible, perhaps three-quarter-round molding could be glued onto the corner, and painted to match the wall. The three-quarter-round could be easily removed if and when you move. Another option is to make a long, narrow (two or three inches wide) banner hanging from a small dowel and covering the corner. Such fabric banners are easy to make and especially lovely if made of silk. If the bedroom is large enough, the poison arrow can be blunted by putting a plant or piece of furniture at the offending corner.

BEDROOMS WITH SLOPING CEILINGS

There is an energetic imbalance if the bedroom ceiling slopes, because the slope will cause a pressurized "crunch" of chi energy at the low end of the room. The solution to this problem is found on page 27. Watch out for exposed beams in bedrooms with sloped ceilings.

CHAPTER ELEVEN

Closets

I am occasionally asked whether a closet is an extension of the bagua of the bedroom. Yes and no. Yes, when the door is open; no, when the door is closed. Closet doors should not be left open on a regular basis, so generally a closet is not an extension. It is its own separate space, but it is too small a room to apply a separate bagua. It does somewhat influence the bagua area of the bedroom that has the closet door.

The first thing to note about a closet is its door.

TYPES OF CLOSET DOORS
Hinged
The hinges of the closet door (as well as any door in the home) must not squeak. If they do, just use some general household oil on them. Squeaky hinges are considered to portend joint problems.

The knob of the closet door must not be able to swing open and actually touch the knob of another door. If this situation exists, use the red ribbons that are described on page 65. You can also take the closet door off and put up curtains, if that works aesthetically.

Sliding doors

If the closet has sliding doors, they should work easily and well. If sliding doors repeatedly come off their tracks, it adds to the frustration level in your life. Fix them, or hire someone to fix them, or remove them and put up curtains.

Curtains

Curtains work fine as closet doors. They give the opportunity to bring in the correct bagua color by the choice of fabric. If the closet is on the entrance wall, use a darker shade of fabric. If the closet door is on the far side of the bedroom (from the entrance) use a bolder and warmer color. See the bagua chapter for color suggestions. One of my clients took down her sliding closet doors and installed an extension rod at the top of the opening. She put curtain-holding clips on the rod. These designer clips resemble shower curtain rings, but they are smaller, and they clip onto the curtain fabric. She had nice curtains with little work.

Unless a fabric is shiny like metal, it brings a yin quality because of its soft flowing nature. Yin is almost always appreciated in a bedroom. Thick, soft fabrics such as velvet are very yin and quite desirable in most bedrooms.

Mirrored doors

Some closet doors are mirrored on the outside. It is widely believed in feng shui that mirrors in the bedroom are problematic. But as with most things in life, some people teach the opposite. Steven Post makes a great case for bedroom mirrors in *The Modern Book of Feng Shui*. (See Recommended Reading.) If you don't have any intuitive or design problems with mirrored closet doors, they may be fine for you. I say, "Judge by how you sleep." You might try covering the doors with fabric for a few weeks, to see if you sleep more soundly. If you sleep just the same, then I doubt the mirrors are affecting you.

If you decide to cover mirrored doors in a bedroom, put up a sturdy rod and hang curtains. The curtains can be very lightweight and need only to be closed when you go to bed. During the day, they can be left open.

ORGANIZATION OF CLOSETS

The organization inside a closet is quite important. Do not store items that you no longer want or use. In *Wind and Water* (see Recommended Reading) Carole Hyder says, "When a closet is jammed full of stuff, the metaphor is that somewhere in your life there's a stagnation and a stuck place that isn't getting loosened. Unload the closet and you'll loosen some aspect of your life."

Color of hangers

Consider having all the clothes hangers a matching color. The color of the hangers should be the correct bagua color for whichever gua within the room the closet door occupies.

If you want to emphasize a particular gua of the bagua of your entire home (based on the front door), look for any closets that fall within that gua. Choose one color for all the bagua hangers in that closet, based on the area of the bagua map in which they reside in your home. The color of the hangers can be based on the color of the bagua, but you have two (possibly different) bagua orientations to choose from, the bagua of your bedroom (based on the entrance) or the bagua of the home as a whole (based on the front door). If you spend a large amount of time in the bedroom, I recommend emphasizing the gua for the bagua of the room. If you live in a medium-sized or large home and can pick colors of hangers for several closets, base the color selection on the larger bagua which overlays the entire home. If it is someone else's bedroom, suggest the appropriate hanger color for their closet location.

Direction of shoes

When shoes are stored in a closet, they should all face the same direction. That way, you are not going against yourself.

CHAPTER TWELVE

Children's Rooms

Children are very important people. Apply the same feng shui principles to your children's rooms as you do to the rest of the home. Children's rooms are extremely important to them and to their development. They do present special feng shui challenges, such as being overly busy.

If you have children living at home, I suggest that you give each of them a bagua map to keep, and explain some principles appropriate to their age and comprehension level. If they have their own rooms, be sure to note things such as an open trash can in a Fortunate Blessings area. Point out what seems appropriate for each child.

Children's rooms should be neat and clean. If children do not learn cleaning and organizing skills at home, they may never learn them. I recommend that children's allowance be partially based on bedroom maintenance. They may not appreciate the discipline at the moment. They will, however, be grateful the rest of their lives as they reap the benefits of good maintenance.

When they are old enough, let them read *Speed Cleaning* and listen to *Getting Organized*. (See Recommended Reading.)

TELEVISIONS AND COMPUTERS

A child or teenager's room is often more than just a place to sleep. For many young people, their bedroom is also a big slice of their world. If there is a television or computer in a child's room, make very sure they do not become a screen junkie at an early age. Proper human development requires the use and exercise of all muscles. People who are hooked on television or computers would benefit from regular swimming or other exercise.

Televisions and computer monitors should be covered at night. This is not always feasible, however. If the children sleep soundly, they are probably not susceptible to the vibration of a media screen. If your child sleeps fretfully, definitely look into covering media screens at night. Any cloth will do, even a T-shirt. But why not make it a nice cloth that the youngster really likes? And while you're at it, use a cloth that is the correct color for the area of the bagua in the bedroom.

A laptop computer is ideal for children's rooms. It is small, easily closed, and has very little electromagnetic radiation.

Children's toys should be put away at night, and they should learn to do it by themselves. Their room will be more peaceful and conducive to sound, restful sleep. If any dolls or plush animals are visible in the room, they may add to a stay awake vibration. Dolls, action figures, and plush animals can be considered to be awake all the time if their eyes can't close. Cover them at night in a cupboard or behind a nice cloth. Not everyone is sensitive to the stay awake vibration. Judge by how soundly the child sleeps. It's certainly all right for the child to take a soft toy to bed.

If the child has or wants an aquarium, it would be best to keep it out of the bedroom. If it must be in the child's bedroom, try to have it in the Fortunate Blessings or Life's Path area of the room. Do not have it near the head of the bed, because it is a fairly active object with bubbles, lights, and moving fish.

I can't imagine a child's room without books. Just be sure that there aren't too many close to the head of the bed or under the bed. Also, don't let the bookcases send a poison arrow or any cutting energy toward the bed. See page 58.

LOCATION

When considering the bagua of the house as a whole, a child's bedroom should not be in the Fortunate Blessings area, as in the following illustration. This sets up a dynamic that the child will run the house. If there is no alternative to having a child's bedroom there, a picture of the parents (or head of the household) should be

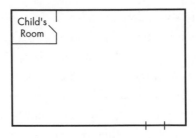

Child's room in the Fortunate Blessing area

on display in that room. This reinstates the parent to a place of empowerment.

If a child's bedroom extends beyond the main body of the house, that child may not feel connected to the rest of the family. This situation and its solution is on page 15.

COLORS

Blue, and especially green, are often recommended for children's bedrooms. These colors represent Wood and signify growth. Yellow is also sometimes recommended, especially if the child needs a bit of grounding. The yellow should be toned down, like mustard, not bright lemon yellow. Beige, off-white, and very light pink are also fine. The main color(s) in the room should not be overly bold and vivid. Children can find enough stimulation in life without their room color screaming at them. However, the room colors should not be too somber. It is fine to have brilliant colors but use them as accents. If the child is overactive, steer away from reds, especially primary red.

Some teenagers want an abundance of black in their room. Black absorbs all other color, and can represent learning and introspection. If your teenager wants to paint the room black, I suggest making an agreement. The teen must do the job alone, do it to your standards, and agree to return it to white when it's time to move out. It will take multiple coats both times. They will have learned valuable painting skills, including prep and cleanup. If you don't want that much black in a bedroom, consider a compromise where just the entrance wall is black. If you are dead set against seeing black in a bedroom, but the teen really wants it, consider black sheets. They are restful, easily available, and you won't usually see them.

BEDS

While I rarely recommend that an adult bed have the long side against a wall, that is okay for a child's bed. In small bedrooms, it allows for more play space. If children share a bedroom, try to have the beds facing the same direction. It brings more harmony. Sheets and bedding with very busy patterns (sports, cartoons, action figures) are not as restful as plain solid colors. Consider using sheets that are the child's favorite color, but not bright red.

Bunk beds should only be used if there is absolutely no alternative. Trundle beds do not usually present a feng shui problem. More information on bunks and trundles is on page 41.

CHAPTER THIRTEEN

Studio Apartments

A studio apartment can be a feng shui powerhouse because the occupant lives primarily in one room. Remember, the more time you spend in a particular room, the more the energy of that space affects you. But the various functions of a studio are often at odds with one another—the busyness of a desk or work area versus the restfulness of a bed.

Studio apartments consist of one main room, plus a bathroom and often, a separate kitchen. The main room is an everything room: living room, bedroom, study, and dining room. Efficiency studios even have the kitchen along one wall. Feng shui likes a separation between different use areas and this is not feasible in most studio apartments. The space limitations just don't permit it. Folding screens are wonderful in studios, if there is adequate space. They provide the needed separation between different use areas. It is especially important that the bed be screened from a desk or work area.

Furniture on wheels is very popular and works great in modern interiors. The wheels on this kind of furniture can be rather large, and make for quick, easy moving. Furniture that moves quickly out of the way when necessary can be a pleasure to live with in a studio apartment, but make sure the furniture is quite stable when not moving. Furniture on wheels always has a yang quality because it can move and is therefore more active. Big wheels are quite yang. Small wheels are almost yin by comparison.

In an ideal studio apartment, the bed disappears when it is not being slept on. A Murphy bed is an example of this. Second best choice would be a bed that is folded into a couch during the day. If the bed must remain in view during the day, try to provide adequate chairs so the bed is seldom used for seating. Of course, in a very small studio the bed is often the only couch. As mentioned on page 50, this is the time to bring on the decorative pillows— any amount, any size; make it like a fancy daybed. The extra pillows should be removed from the bed when sleeping. Their purpose is to define the bed as a couch when they're on, and as a bed when they're removed. Add any other decorative fabric throw that appeals to you such as a bed scarf or afghan. The color and shape of the pillows can emphasize the correct element for their placement in the room. For instance, if the bed is in the Children and Creativity gua, try round white pillows with silver metallic threads in a brocade fabric.

DESK WORK

When there is no desk in the studio, desk work is often done at a dining table or coffee table. If this is the case, be sure to clear away the desk work when done. Left out, it will likely be the beginning of a pileup of clutter. When the desk work is put away, the table resumes its original function and serenity reigns in the room.

If there is a desk in the studio, make sure you can see the entrance door when working. Use a mirror if necessary. It is fine to leave standard desk items in view such as a pen and pencil holder or letter tray. But try not to leave paperwork in progress in view all the time. A desk like that is calling you to come and finish the project. We don't need our furniture to be talking to us, especially in the room where we sleep. If a computer is used, go for a laptop that can be easily closed and put away.

Because of the concentrated work done on a desk surface, it can have a bagua grid applied to it. The entrance side is at the desk chair. The Fortunate Blessings area is the far left corner when you are seated. Appropriate things to put there are: A computer (it's expensive), a vase of flowers or a living plant, an elegant paperweight, or any desk items that are blue, purple, or red. Do not let this area become cluttered or messy. Refer to the principles on page 94, to enhance any other bagua areas of the desk. Be sure not to keep things that could cut (scissors, stapler, tape dispenser) in the Relationship area of the desk. A more subtle way to enhance the bagua areas of the desk is to tape colored paper under the desktop. The paper can be cut to the shape of the element for the specific gua. Examples are a red triangle for the Fame area or a foil circle for the Children and Creativity area. The paper cutouts would look quite funky on the desktop, but underneath, no one will see them. You know they're there because you put them there. They're working for you.

OTHER CONSIDERATIONS

Clutter is a hazard in any bedroom. In a studio apartment it is a severe liability. It is causing chaos and stagnation in the resident's life. Clutter is a self-imposed problem. Reread the section on Clutter, on page 81, and take it to heart. If you live in a studio apartment, you must restrict the number of things you own. The items that surround you can be beautiful, but first they should be functional.

A fountain may not seem functional, but if it's in the Fortunate Blessings area of the apartment, it will be functioning for you. You will probably want to turn it off at night. Use a timer if that's more convenient.

If you can place a doormat outside your studio apartment, do so. Make sure that it contains some red or even is completely red. It will be acting as a stop sign saying to the chi energy, "Stop! Come in here." A red tassel on your outside door knob will do the same thing.

CHAPTER FOURTEEN

Guestrooms and Other Special Bedrooms

GUEST ROOMS

A guest room is quite handy, but if it is used infrequently, it can impart a stagnant energy to the home. Check the bagua for the entire home to see what aspect of your life corresponds to that room. The most problematic area for a guestroom is in the Fortunate Blessings corner. It gives the guests too much power in the household, it's a problem if they don't keep the room neat, and it can even be a problem when no one is visiting. The Fortunate Blessings area of the home should never feel stagnant. It should seem alive and vibrant.

Any guest room benefits from enhancements that liven it up. Such things could include a faceted lead crystal, especially in a window that receives direct sunlight, a wind chime, especially near a window that is occasionally opened for fresh air, or a small decorative light that comes on for a few hours each evening. It is especially good if the light is visible to someone passing by the room. You can also put a fountain which runs all the time in the guest room. Put the fountain in the Fortunate Blessings corner of the room if possible. It is fine for guests to turn the fountain off when they are staying there. The easiest way to do this is by installing an on/off switch that the fountain plugs into.

If possible, keep the guest room door open when no one is staying there. A closed-up room always says "stagnant." A guest room is, of course, less stagnant if it is a multipurpose room—doubling as an office or a workroom. If the guest room also functions as an office, cover any monitor screens while guests are there. Laptops with their closeable screens are ideal.

If there is no separate guest room and the guests must sleep on a sofa bed in a more public room, be considerate of their needs. Try to provide ample closet, cabinet, or drawer space so they don't have to leave their things in view. If household members need to pass through the room while guests are there, use folding screens (or something similar) to partition off a more private area.

When you are a guest in someone's home, be aware of poison arrows that aim across the bed. Cover them when going to bed, but remove the coverings when you arise. That way you won't inadvertently cause your host to feel uncomfortable or think of your behavior as strange and ungrateful. When you return home, send the hosts a thank you note.

We are all guests on planet Earth. In the same sense, you are a guest in the home that shelters you. Be grateful for your home and your bedroom. Occasionally say to your bedroom that you appreciate it and are grateful to it. This is not a silly thing to do. Rather, it is a verbal expression of what should be a constant attitude of gratitude. Both you and your bedroom will benefit from the expression.

HOTEL ROOMS

When staying in public lodging, ask for a room in the rear half of the building, away from the elevator. If any of the furniture (side tables or dressers, for example) aims a poison arrow across the bed, cover the offending corner when sleeping. You can also cover the television screen when it is not in use. Keep the bathroom door closed when sleeping. Hotel rooms are an excellent place to use aromatherapy.

SLEEPING OUTSIDE

Sleeping porches

Sleeping porches became popular at the beginning of the twentieth century. Of course, people in warm climates frequently kept a bed on the back porch for use on hot summer nights. Sleeping porches gained popularity in the early 1900s because of the Arts and Crafts movement. They were often a feature (usually on the second floor) of Craftsman houses. They provided an opportunity to get plenty of fresh air while sleeping. Part of the Arts and Crafts philosophy was aimed to foster a return to simpler, more natural way of life.

Breathing fresh air while sleeping is certainly laudable, but the degree of openness on a porch is not conducive to deep rest. If you wish to use your sleeping porch, try to make it feel a bit more enclosed. Open or screened sides should preferably have a solid half-wall up to waist height. Some tall potted plants along the open walls can also help enclose and define a space. The head of the bed should be against a solid wall. Often the only solid wall is the one with the doorway into the house. This places the bed in a disempowered position, so a mirror should be positioned on the opposite wall. That wall may consist of only a few support posts, so attach a mirror to one of them. A convex mirror may be the best option, or even a gazing ball. See page 24. If the bed cannot be placed against a solid wall, it must have a large, solid, headboard.

Camping

Some tents have structural support bars that are visible inside. These are usually not of great concern in modern tents, which use tensile strength for their structure. There is no pressure down on the support bars , unlike the structural beams in a building. If the support bars really do hold something up, such as in old-fashioned pup tents, try to pin some fabric over the support bar. It never hurts to cover support bars in any tent, especially if you will be there for more than three nights. A tree that is directly outside a tent door should be at least six feet away.

Foam pads are preferred over air mattresses, because of the pressurized vibration of the air mattress. Who wants a vacation with pressure vibes! When tent camping, sleep with your head away from the door of the tent.

When sleeping in the great outdoors with no tent, you're going to get some great fresh air, but you're not likely to get great sleep. It's okay occasionally, such as when you are watching meteor showers, but not on a regular basis. Even something as simple as a mosquito net will allow your rest to be deeper.

ROOMS FOR THE SICK

If someone is bedridden, make sure there is green in the room. It is relaxing and represents healing. There should be adequate air circulation (preferably fresh air). A sick person appreciates peace and quiet. Bring fresh chi to them by touching or massaging them. Too many sick people only have contact with a remote control.

CHAPTER FIFTEEN

Adjacent Bathrooms

A large number of bedrooms either have a bathroom attached or share a wall with a bathroom. If the bathroom opens immediately into the bedroom there must be a door between the two rooms. That door must be closed at night. The wetness and heaviness of the bathroom should not influence the energy of the bedroom while someone is sleeping. If there is an en suite bathroom with no door between the two rooms, add a door or curtains. It is better to keep the curtains and any bathroom door closed most of the time. That way the drain vibration doesn't seep into the rest of the home. It is also good to have a mirror on the outside of the bathroom door and/or a mirror above the door (on the outside). The mirrors repel chi from entering the bathroom.

Laying down a bagua for a regular-sized bathroom is a losing proposition. The space is just to small to make effective statements for each of the nine areas. Instead, look at where the bathroom is within the bagua of the whole home. If the bathroom is in the Creativity area of the whole home, go for chrome and pastels. If it is in the Relationship area of the home, go for pinks, reds, and whites, and groupings of things. A bathroom in the Fortunate Blessings area should look royal, lots of purple, blue, gold, or red, and it should be ultra-neat and clean. Use the appropriate bagua colors, depending on where the bathroom is in the house. Bring in those colors with such things as towels, bath mats, shower curtain, soap dish, or soap squirter.

DRAINS

The bathroom is the most problematic room in the house according to feng shui. This is largely because of the drains. A standard bathroom has at least three drains, often more. Each of those drains is an opportunity for chi to drain down and out of your life. To keep chi from draining away, keep the drains covered as much as possible.

Sink drains

Sink drains often have a built-in metal stopper that hides most of the actual drain hole. These are great, because all you see is a tiny sliver of the drain hole. Also, the reflective stopper repels chi away from the drain. Don't let that stopper get grimy! It's quite easy to close the drains all the way.

If the sink is older, it probably doesn't have a built-in metal stopper. These sinks benefit from having a hair-catching strainer. It reduces the size of the drain hole. It's inconvenient to keep moving the stopper every time the sink is used. If you don't mind, do it. If you do mind, at least use a strainer.

Tub and shower drains

Tub and shower drains can be dealt with in either of the above ways. In addition, keep the shower curtain or door pulled so the wash area isn't seen. If it needs to remain partly open, the part that is seen should be away from the drain.

Toilet

The toilet is the most offensive drain in the home. This is partly because of what happens there, but mostly because of the drain hole's size. It is the largest drain hole in the home. The toilet drain is so easy to hide—just keep the lid down when it's not in use. It is much more important to keep the toilet lid down than to keep sink and tub drains plugged. Develop the habit yourself, but do not harangue your guests. Close the lid before flushing.

There are two other ways to prevent chi from draining away. Put a very large round rock on the floor directly behind the toilet. The rock should be round, because it will need to be wiped clean occasionally, and it should be large because it is acting as a grounding object. It's big, it's heavy, it ain't goin' anywhere. The rock should be too large to flush down the toilet. This counters the flush and drain vibration of the toilet. It can also be used at the drain end of a claw-foot tub or under a sink. If the bathroom has a ceramic tile floor, put felt on the bottom of the rock to avoid damaging the tile.

Snake plant (Sansevieria) can be used effectively around the toilet or tub to counter the drain down vibrations. Its strong uprising form says "no" to the down-and-out vibrations very effectively. Place it in pots on the floor on each side of the toilet tank. Snug the pots right up against the wall, as far under the tank as they can go without bending the leaves. If your tank is out from the wall a bit, you might even have leaves coming up from behind the tank. Don't have any of the leaves terribly close to the seat. A pot of Sansevieria can also be placed on top of the toilet tank or near any bathroom drain.

It is best if the toilet is not reflected in a mirror, because that symbolically doubles the number of toilets. Do not keep a plunger in view next to the toilet. The plunger says "dysfunctional toilet." Store it away in a cabinet or closet. If the plunger is used frequently, call a plumber and deal with the more fundamental drainage problem.

MOIST ENERGY

A bathroom is a very yin room. It has no stove or oven to help balance the several areas of wetness (tub, shower, sinks, and toilet). If a bathroom is visually busy or complicated, this pushes the yin component off the scale, and the room becomes unbalanced and unhealthy. There are many ways to add yang to a bathroom, thereby making it more balanced energetically. It will then be healthier for the nearby rooms.

Add plants. Real or artificial plants are quite appropriate in a bathroom. Real plants appreciate the humidity and use it to build their plant bodies. They are symbolically converting the excess of water in that room into their leaves and stems. Pictures of plants are also good.

Have proper ventilation. The healthiest bathrooms are those with windows that open. Use the window regularly to ventilate and air out the bathroom. Nothing can beat fresh air. If there is no window, you may have the beginning of an unhealthy bathroom. If mildew grows in your bathroom, deal with it. Mildew equals an unhealthy situation. Clean it (all) out. (See *Speed Cleaning* in Recommended Reading.) Keep the ventilating fan on all the time when you are gone. You may choose not to keep the ventilating fan on very much when you are home because of the sound, but when you are leaving, turn the fan on. The ventilation will dry the bathroom (making it more yang), and mildew will not regrow (eliminating the excessively yin "rot" vibration.)

Fresh air is best, and direct sunlight is ideal. It can totally eliminate a dank smell, which should not just be masked. Pleasant fragrance is appreciated in a bathroom, but it cannot replace fresh air. For most of humanity's history, bathrooms have been outbuildings that didn't influence the main living space. Modern plumbing (a comparatively recent invention) allows bathrooms to be anywhere. If the bathroom is situated with an outside window, it retains some of that removed, outside connection and doesn't influence the rooms around it as much.

Add red to represent Fire. The vibration of Fire is uprising and it lifts the drain vibe of the bathroom. It is usually more appropriate to represent Fire with color than with shape in the bathroom, because angular objects can seem unfriendly in such a small room. Red does not have to be the main theme color, but it should be there somewhere. It's fine to use plenty of red if that works in the decor. Green and/or blue can be used if red is completely inappropriate. They represent Wood, which feeds Fire. Candles are good in bathrooms.

Keep it simple almost to the point of austere. Don't use patterned wallpaper or a patterned shower curtain. Avoid tchotchkes, knickknacks, and clutter of any kind in this room. A bathroom can be elegant and feel wonderful by simply using color as the unifying theme.

Keep fabric to a minimum because it is a yin material. Use natural fabrics for towels, washcloths, and rugs, but avoid any other fabric use if possible. It's okay to use a fabric shower curtain, but it should dry quickly. Do not use a shower liner and a shower curtain. It's too much fabric and it's too fussy. If you can achieve window privacy without curtains, don't use them.

Don't use water imagery. It's fine for a bathroom to have a picture or two, but there should not be any water in the picture. Also don't decorate with seashells or images of fish, dolphins, or other such creatures. Those things say "water."

CHAPTER SIXTEEN

Implementation of What You've Learned

PRIORITIES FOR MAKING FENG SHUI CHANGES

The first priority is to listen to your intuition. If certain feng shui changes are screaming to be done (and can be done quickly), then do them. Common sense goes hand-in-hand with intuition. Keep them alive in your life by acting on them.

The second priority is to eliminate outside influences. Use mirrors outside of any window or door that has a foreboding object pointing at it. See page 60.

The third priority is to clean your bedroom thoroughly and well, including the windows if they need it. Then continue to clean it well on a regular basis. Make it easy by doing it the professional way, as taught in *Speed Cleaning*. (See Recommended Reading.) If you don't already have the habit of making your bed each morning, do so.

Once you've cleaned your bedroom thoroughly, consider painting the walls or ceiling. If you've always had white walls, you'll be amazed at the positive change of adding a favorite color. You don't have to paint all the walls, and you can always paint over it if you don't like the new color or when you leave (if you're a renter). On my advice, one of my clients painted the far wall of her bedroom red. She used a very rich, sophisticated color between dark maroon and crimson. Her large wooden headboard was then placed against the center of the wall. The effect was stunning. When she was in bed, she saw the three white walls, but when she opened the door to come into her bedroom, there was the beautiful red. She said, "I realize how it affects chi energy because when I see it I am pulled into the room." Some feng shui teachers advise against blue or green walls in a relationship bedroom, because they are cool colors. They can symbolize a chilled relationship.

Next, find out if there are any missing areas and bring them back with mirrors or other ways. See page 114.

After that, empower yourself by making sure that you can see the door from the bed and/or desk. See page 24.

Now is the time to deal with clutter if you haven't already. If you are awash in clutter, make time for organizing. Make it a priority. Clutter can stop everything. Even if your stuff seems well-organized, if there's too much of it, you will be blocking your feng shui success. Please take this seriously and trim your possessions back to what is truly useful in your life right now. Once the decision has been made to get rid of an object, carry out the decision quickly. As mentioned on page 83, start near the doorway and in the Fortunate Blessings corner.

Once the clutter is gone, apply the bagua. If certain life areas are more important right now, emphasize them first. I generally recommend beginning with the Fortunate Blessings area, because it represents intention. Things that might be seen as coincidences can be the Universe responding to your request via the bagua.

SPACE CLEARING

Space clearing is not a priority or even a necessity for everyone. However, if the bedroom has never had any type of vibrational cleansing, please consider it. This is especially important if someone has died in the room, or if it was once a relationship bedroom and the relationship has ended. (In that case, you should consider getting a different bed.)

Most of a space clearing is accomplished by a thorough cleaning from ceiling to floor. Pay special attention to the carpet or rugs. Just as dirt can settle in there, so can old vibes. Here are a few tips for space clearing. Yes, you can do it yourself! In fact, it's probably more powerful if you do it yourself.

- Don't do it at night.
- Have every window open as fully as possible. Let the natural breezes do some of the work for you.
- Go around the entire inside perimeter of the bedroom, including closets. Go in a clockwise direction, which means turning to your left as soon as you have entered the room.
- Carry burning incense or a sage smudge bundle (see Glossary).
- If possible, carry a pure-sounding bell, and ring it every few steps. If someone is assisting you, one can carry the incense, and the other can carry the bell.
- If no bell is readily available, use your hands and clap. Don't clap as if you were applauding. Do single, loud, sharp claps when you get to corners and doorways and any place that feels a little unusual—any kind of unusual. It is an extremely powerful, assertive thing to do. You are using your own hands to claim your rightful ownership of a space. Clap high and clap low. You cannot clap and hold incense at the same time, so if you are doing this alone, you will have to make two complete circuits. If you have time, go ahead and make a third circuit. You cannot overdo it, and three is a very powerful number.

- Sing, chant, or speak aloud, whichever you are most comfortable with. The very ancient chant "Om" is always appropriate. Anything that you feel expresses your intention is appropriate. You could simply say, "Peace to this room," over and over. There are some instances when your voice should sound assertive and rather loud. If the room or home has a troubled history, or has an unsettled feel in any way, you should say things like, "Get out!" or "Scat!" like you really mean it. Say it as if you are shooing out an unwelcome cat.
- Be sure the smoke from the incense wafts high and low. Bring the incense near the floor and the ceiling, in every corner, including closets and cabinets. Open drawers and cabinet doors. Move the incense all around every object in the room, including under the bed. Do an ultra-thorough job. It may take a while, but you are not likely to be doing it very often.
- These are the good times to do a space clearing. When you first move in, on your birthday, and on Chinese New Year.

RECOMMENDED READING

FENG SHUI BOOKS

Feng Shui Demystified
by Clear Englebert
190 Pages. The Crossing Press, Freedom, California, 2000

This book jumps right in with information on how to do feng shui effectively. It does not dwell on such things as the history of feng shui. When a problem is described, multiple solutions are always suggested. I realize you can't just move if something is wrong with your home. There is always a way to fix a bad situation (no matter how ornery) and in a way that will fit with your decor. I've tried to be especially sensitive to renters, who have less control over their abode than home owners.

Feng Shui House Book
by Gina Lazenby and William Spear
160 Pages. Watson-Guptill, New York, 1998

More feng shui books with color photographs are being published. They are usually pricey and often not worth the money. This book is well worth the price. The pictures are a feng shui education. It stands head and shoulders above other feng shui books with color photographs, because of Lazenby's extensive commentary. She does what almost no other author does, she comments on everything in the picture. It's frustratingly common to find feng shui books illustrated with pictures full of poison arrow beams, et cetera, and the author's only comment is on the color of the couch. This is such a disservice because readers might think that the beams (or dark ceiling fan, for example) are somehow okay because nothing is said to the contrary. Lazenby does the opposite. She goes the extra mile by even pointing out what can be done to improve the situation. Her writing is power-packed. She can say in one sentence what some authors require a paragraph for. Even the structure of the chapters is a breath of fresh air.

There is a condensed version of this book, called *Simple Feng Shui* by Gina Lazenby. The print is sometimes quite small, but it is considerably cheaper.

Modern Book of Feng Shui
by Steven Post
241 Pages. Dell Publishing, New York, 1998

There is an abundance of information in this book written by the first American teacher of feng shui. If you are looking for an excuse to keep mirrors in the bedroom, read page 68 and rest easy. He includes a well-illustrated section on blessings and rituals and full instructions for using a bagua based on the entrance.

Move your Stuff, Change your Life
by Karen Rauch Carter
233 Pages. Simon & Schuster, New York, 2000

This book conveys serious life-changing information in a light-hearted way. Carter's jovial tone keeps you happily turning pages all the way to the end. The book contains a hefty chapter for each area of the bagua. These nine chapters contain what you need to know about feng shui in general, such as poison arrows and elemental cycles. What isn't covered there is dealt with in the final two chapters. The author is refreshingly forthright, and so are the drawings.

Practical Feng Shui
by Simon Brown
160 Pages. Sterling Publishing Company, New York, 1997

This is one of the finest feng shui books ever written. All aspects of Compass feng shui are explained and illustrated. Brown explains more stuff more clearly, than any other author. The charts and illustrations are also the best I've seen. A beginner will not get lost or bogged down, and the more advanced feng shui reader will appreciate how much is packed into this powerful book. *Practical Feng Shui* will probably be one of your most referred-to feng shui books. I recommend this book for everyone.

Western Guide to Feng Shui
by Terah Kathryn Collins
253 Pages. Hay House, Carlsbad, California, 1997

The text is complete and supplemented with truly excellent graphics. Her writing is lucid, making it very accessible for beginners. The chapters on individual guas include numerous suggestions for affirmations. There is also an audiotape set available from the same publisher.

Wind and Water: Your Personal Feng Shui Journey
by Carole J. Hyder
257 Pages. The Crossing Press, Freedom, California, 1999

The style of this book is somewhat unique for a feng shui book. No section is more than one page long, and each is chock full of introspective knowledge. It is as if you are reading aphorisms or daily reminders. Her approach is powerful and will allow the reader to understand more deeply what feng shui changes are all about. It is also available as a four-tape set from The Crossing Press.

BOOKS ON RELATED TOPICS

Clutter Control
by Jeff Campbell
159 Pages. Dell Publishing, New York, 1992

One of the things I like best about Jeff Campbell's books is that he lays down the rules for handling clutter early on:

Use it or lose it. The exact words you will hear from many a feng shui teacher.

Use a file cabinet. He makes a big case for hanging files, and I agree completely.

Items displayed in the house have to pass a test. "After all, you only have so much space. The items taking up that space should justify themselves. It's not a complicated test. They just have to have a valid reason for being there."

Label things. Including (but not limited to) all storage boxes.

The second chapter, "The Psychology of Clutter," is quite powerful. Here Campbell tackles the three most common excuses used by packrats. 1) "I might need it someday." 2) "They don't make them like this any more." 3) "It reminds me of someone I love or someplace I've been." One-by-one he offers rebuttals to those rationalizations. The bulk of the book is devoted to a huge alphabetical list of places to de-clutter (cupboards, closets…) and particular things (paper, photographs, keys…) This is an extremely useful book. If your home is less cluttered, it will not only be easier to clean, it will also help you reach your goals (rather than work against you)!

Dream Book
by Betty Bethards
174 Pages. Inner Light Foundation, Petaluma, California, 1993.

This is the best dream dictionary ever published, plus there is ample information on how to decode a dream. There is a separate audiotape, *Dreams*, which is also the best of its kind. Learning to listen to what our dreams are telling us is one of the most powerful things a person can do. The book and the tape are a great combination.

Getting Organized
by Stephanie Winston
Audiotape, 54 minutes. Simon & Schuster, 1986.

Organization is basic to feng shui, but saying it and doing it are two very different things! For some people, to be organized is a major lifestyle challenge. The outcome can seem attractive, but getting from here to there can be daunting. The good news is that the tape version of *Getting Organized* can seep into you like osmosis. Keep listening to it until you are doing all of it. Stephanie Winston covers every aspect of being organized. Her voice is so confident, she will get you there. The best advice I can give anyone who wants to be better organized is to listen to Stephanie Winston. I've read scores of organizing books, and this one stands high—especially the tape version.

Kevin McCloud's Lighting Style
by Kevin McCloud
144 Pages. Simon and Schuster, New York, 1995.

I have owned three bookstores and have seen a multitude of books on lighting. I think *Lighting Style* is the best, because McCloud teaches and you learn. There is a wealth of information presented with brilliant illustrations. He shows the same room with different kinds of lighting and you can really see the effects. I especially appreciated the section at the end of the book explaining the different kinds of light bulbs. This book is of enduring value.

Speed Cleaning
by Jeff Campbell
119 pages. Dell, New York, 1987.

Cleaning is as essential to feng shui as breathing is to life. This is by far the best book on cleaning ever published. It should be taught in schools, because sooner or later everybody has to do some cleaning. You may as well be smart about it. As in feng shui, this book isn't afraid to state the obvious. Some rules are shockingly simple, as in, "work from top to bottom," "if it isn't dirty, don't clean it," and "pay attention," but when applied together, they make for fast, excellent cleaning.

Winning Windows
by Judy Sheridan
96 pages. Random House, New York, 1996.

There are many fine books available on window treatments. *Winning Windows* is one of them. The book is composed of case studies, complete with drawings and photographs. Most importantly, Sheridan explains the thinking that preceded the design. This truly empowers readers with the necessary knowledge so that they can approach their own window challenges. Sheridan is excellent at showing how details can complete a look. Many of the windows will seem overly fussy to some people, but the vast amount of fabric involved is quite perfect for bedrooms because of its yin quality. Not all the window treatments are overblown. Some are refreshingly simple, such as Roman shades or balloon shades.

GLOSSARY

Bullnose corners

These are premolded drywall beads that form a radius instead of making a sharp right angle. They are applied after the Sheetrock but before mudding. They can also be installed at any time. Check the telephone directory under drywall supplies.

Chi

Pronounced chee. The basic energy of the Universe.

Elements

There are five elements according to Taoism: Water, Wood, Fire, Metal, and Earth. (The word "Element" here has nothing to do with the Periodic Table of Western science.) Taoism refers to archetypal energies. Everything in the Universe is considered to be an expression of one of the Elements.

Gua or Guas

The Chinese name for any of the eight non-central bagua areas. Guas is the plural. See page 93.

I Ching

The *I Ching* is an ancient Chinese oracle, considered by many to be the oldest book in the world.

Magnetic sleep pad

A pad with magnets in it, which usually goes under the mattress, providing an even, negative, magnetic field for your body. There are several reputable manufacturers. One is Magnetico, in Calgary, Alberta, Canada (800-265-1119, www.magneticosleep.com).

Poison arrow

This (malevolent) chi energy has various names: sha chi, or shar. It is chi energy that has encountered something in the environment to cause it to speed up or get irritated. See page 54.

Sage Smudge Stick

This is sometimes called a sage wand. It is a tightly bound bundle of dried sage stems and leaves. Usually wild sage is used. It is lit at the tip end, and then the flame is extinguished (usually by waving it rapidly rather than by using one's breath.) It continues to smolder, and makes a lot of smoke. You'll probably want to temporarily disable the smoke alarm in the room before using it. You have to fan it or blow on it occasionally to keep it smoldering. Sage smudging is a Native American technique. It's messier than incense because it drops bits of black ash around the room. It is a powerful tool for eliminating negative vibrations, but use it with an awareness of fire safety. One incense company makes a sage incense of superior quality: Botanical Creations in Gardner, Colorado.

Trigram

The basic unit of a trigram is a line, either solid or with an opening, like two dashes.

When combined in units of three lines, there are only eight possible combinations. They are listed on the Chart of Bagua Areas on page 111 with their meanings.

A solid yang line   An open yin line

Wind catcher

A wind catcher is any kind of silent decorative object that hangs outside and moves in the wind. They are especially useful in situations where the sound of a wind chime would be annoying. Some windcatchers are simply colorful threads that dangle.

BOOKS BY THE CROSSING PRESS

Feng Shui Demystified

by Clear Englebert

A concise, inexpensive guide to the ancient principles of feng shui for the home, office, and garden. Author Clear Englebert explains the differences in feng shui variations and then discusses how to put the art into practice. This guide enables anyone to practice feng shui for a more peaceful and harmonious home environment. The book also includes a separate full-color bagua, one of feng shui's most powerful tools.

$10.95 • Paper • ISBN 1-58091-078-5

Fundamentals of Tibetan Buddhism

by Rebecca McClen Novick

This book explores the history, philosophy, and practice of Tibetan Buddhism. Novick's concise history of Buddhism, and her explanations of the Four Noble Truths, Wheel of Life, Karma, Five Paths, Six Perfections, and the different schools of thought within the Buddhist teachings help us understand Tibetan Buddhism as a way of experiencing the world, more than as a religion or philosophy.

$12.95 • Paper • ISBN 0-89594-953-9

BOOKS BY THE CROSSING PRESS

Living Feng Shui: Personal Stories

by Carole J. Hyder

The case study format allows you to see how feng shui can enhance your life and the floor plans allow you to follow the application of Feng Shui principles. These elements combine to provide a clear concept and appreciation of feng shui.
—Deborah Sures, feng shui consultant and interior designer

$19.95 • Paper • ISBN 1-58091-115-3

Wind and Water: Your Personal Feng Shui Journey

by Carole J. Hyder

This book presents feng shui as simple suggestions that can be done on a daily basis—each page provides information and a corresponding activity. Instead of just reading about it in the abstract, this book gives you an immediate experience of feng shui.

$19.95 • Paper • ISBN 1-58091-050-5

To receive a current catalog from The Crossing Press,
call us toll-free at 1.800.777.1048
or visit our Web site at **www. crossingpress.com**

www.crossingpress.com

BROWSE through the Crossing Press Web site for information on upcoming titles, new releases, and backlist books including brief summaries, excerpts, author information, reviews, and more.

SHOP our store for all of our books and, coming soon, unusual, interesting, and hard-to-find sideline items related to Crossing's best-selling books!

READ informative articles by Crossing Press authors on all of our major topics of interest.

SIGN UP for our e-mail newsletter to receive late-breaking developments and special promotions from The Crossing Press.